THE GUINEA PIGS

Ludvík Vaculík was born in Brumov/Mahren, Czechoslovakia, in 1926. As a young man, he was an apprentice shoemaker and attended the Special School for Foreign Commerce in Zlin. After World War II, he studied at the University for Political Science and Sociology in Prague. He was an editor of *Literární Noviny* (*Literary Newspaper*) and *Literární Listy* (*Literary Information Sheet*) until his work was banned on August 21, 1968—a punishment for the famous "Two Thousand Word Manifesto" written earlier that year. Outcast and destitute, Vaculík now lives in Prague with his wife and two sons. *The Guinea Pigs* was the first of his books to appear in English, followed by *The Axe*.

LUDVÍK VACULÍK

THE
GUINEA PIGS

Translated by Káča Poláčková

Introduction by Neal Ascherson

Northwestern University Press
Evanston, Illinois

Originally published as *Die Meerschweinchen*
by Verlag C. J. Bucher, Lucerne, Switzerland, 1971
First published in the United States by The Third Press,
Joseph Okpaku Publishing Co., Inc., 1973
Published by Penguin Books Inc., 1975
Northwestern University Press Paperback edition, 1986
by arrangement with Penguin Books Inc.

Translated from the unpublished Czech original *Morčata*,
by arrangement with Verlag C. J. Bucher,
publishers of the German edition, *Die Meerschweinchen*
Northwestern University Press Paperback edition published 1986 by
Northwestern University Press, Evanston, IL 60201

First Printing

Printed and bound in the United States of America

Library of Congress Catalog Card Number: 86-061248
ISBN: 0-8101-0726-0

Introduction

"Writing is always somehow an expression of powerlessness, or the fruit of frayed nerves; it betrays complexes, or a bad conscience." So says the central figure of *The Guinea Pigs,* a Prague bank clerk lowering himself into that timeless, cozy bath of petty-bourgeois reflections on art: no harm in it as a hobby or even as a regular source of income, as long as you stay in the bounds of healthy entertainment; once writers start giving themselves airs, though . . . .

Ludvík Vaculík himself gives the opposite impression. Stout, patient, ironic, and once he has decided to start talking, much inclined to go on, Vaculík generates plenty of power through well-insulated nerves. He and Milan Kundera are the leading prose writers in Czech alive today, although neither of them is allowed to publish in his own country. This novel, completed in Prague in 1970, has not appeared in Czech or Slovak bookshops, and for the foreseeable future there is no prospect that it will. Kundera is leaving for France. Vaculík, with no job and only the money from Western sales, which trickles past various dams and weirs erected by the bureaucracy across his bank account, prefers to stay. On the one hand, nobody is actually trying to lock him up or to draft him to do window-cleaning. On the other hand, what he has to say to the French and the Germans and the Americans is limited, or so he feels. Inside Vaculík there is an obstinate fear that if he leaves his country, he will lose his vision; he has a sense of buried cables of communication between man and land which—once snapped—cannot be reconnected again. So he stays. "These acquaintances, they ask me how I am. I reply that I can't complain. I wouldn't know where to."

After the Czech wave in the cinema, which made Miloš Forman, Ivan Passer, Jiri Menzel, and Jan Němec so famous in the West and eventually washed many of them up there, came the Czech novels. Josef Škvorecký's *The Cowards*, Kundera's *The Joke* and *Life Is Elsewhere*, and Vaculík's *The Axe* and *The Guinea Pigs* have appeared in English, French, and German translations in the last few years, and there are many more. These novels, written before and after the "Prague spring" and the Soviet invasion, form a unique body in contemporary European fiction, and yet they form nothing like a "wave." They emerge from a common literary tradition and intellectual heritage, but it is a tradition wide enough to contain great oppositions and contrasts.

Czech writing, in this century at least, has been possessed by two main fascinations. One is a humanist, "Western" moral curiosity, the feelings of a small and reasoning people subjected to greater, clumsier powers—Austria-Hungary, Nazi Germany, and now the Soviet Union—who try to impose a view of life which is emptily heroic and dingily superstitious. The spectacle can be comic, as the Good Soldier Schweik trudges about Bohemia hoping to please. It can also be tragic: The young poet in Kundera's *Life Is Elsewhere* is tempted, in his ambition to become a burning Shelley of the revolution, into betraying every moral law and ignoring every fundamental truth. In either mode, however, and reinforced by the socialist ideals that even today come naturally to Czech and Slovak intellectuals, there is insistence that human life is various, that all commanders are fallible, and that all ideologies must fail which ignore the erratic and the casual and the spontaneous in the citizen's behavior.

Ester Krumbachová, who wrote some of the best film scripts of the sixties, once tried to illustrate this irrepressible moral curiosity by telling a fable. You feed a sparrow and feel good—until a cat eats the sparrow and you feel outraged—until you find that the cat was starving and the sparrow was caught only because he was too fat to move. Then a man at a window, watching the scene, lifts a gun and blows the cat to bits. "Morally, he was obviously in the right. But you go over and ask him why he shot the cat, and you may find out that he'd just bought a new gun and was itching to try it out. Or perhaps he was simply a sadist. You see, this is the sort of theme which interests me" (from Antonin J. Liehm, *The Politics of Culture* [New York: Grove Press, Inc., 1972]). The philosopher Karel Kosík takes the theme further: "A man who has no conscience, who doesn't die, who cannot laugh, who is unaware of personal responsibility—such a man is of course the perfect unit needed in a manipulated, bureaucratically regimented system."

This is where the second, darker fascination of Czech fiction comes in. Sometimes this "perfect unit" appears as a literally artificial man: the clay golem fashioned by the cabalist Rabbi Löw, the robots of Karel Čapek, the profusion of humanoid automatons in Czech trick-films. Sometimes it is the other way around: In a sinister, swimming mist of uncertainty, all the denser as the manipulators themselves gain in certainty, we see human beings losing their conscience, their responsibility, and their sense of mortality as they degenerate quietly into those mechanical "perfect units." Jan Němec's film *The Party and the Guests* conveyed such an atmosphere. *The Guinea Pigs* does the same.

It is not that these two fascinations are mutually exclusive. They are inseparably connected through the Czech experience. They occur, in different proportions, in the work of each good writer. Thus the difference between Kundera, a "classical" psychological novelist comparable at his best to Gustave Flaubert, and Vaculík, with his stronger feeling for deep social determinants of human behavior and his more Central European taste for mystery, is not the polarity between Ivan Turgenev and Fëdor Dostoevski. *Life Is Elsewhere* displays several characters who, as one of the victims of the Slánský trials said of himself, are quite normal except that they have ceased to be human beings; and Vaculík, in 1968 and the years before, played democratic politics with energy and optimism (his famous declaration, the "Two Thousand Words" of June 1968, must be the only national manifesto to contain jokes). With *The Guinea Pigs,* however, Vaculík has firmly shifted over toward those darker and more sinister preoccupations.

Ludvík Vaculík is not from Prague or from the older intellectual classes. He was born in a village in the hills of Moravia, and his father was a small farmer (to the Czech reader, it seems that Vaculík retains a particularly Moravian use of words which escapes translation). He was trained as a shoemaker but made his way to the University for Political Science and Sociology in Prague immediately after the war. After eight years as a teacher of apprentices Vaculík became a journalist and worked for radio and later for magazines. His first novel, *The Busy House,* came out in 1963, but it was *The Axe,* published in 1966, which made him famous. This is the story—much drawn from his own life—of a lonely farmer who deliberately destroys his own family relationships and friendships to bring socialist collectivization to his village in Moravia and who—through the very challenge that his own integrity offers to the corrupt Stalinist bureaucracy of the new order—is himself in the end destroyed.

From then onward, Vaculík was one of the leaders of the Writers' Union in its battle against the decaying authority of the Antonin Novotný regime. He was an editor of *Literární Noviny* and *Literární Listy,* the mouthpieces of the reformers in the Writers' Union, and in 1967, at the famous congress of the union which brought its members into head-on collision with Novotný's cultural managers, he made a speech that was not just an attack on censorship but the deadliest attack on the abuse of political power which the regime had ever heard. With several colleagues, Vaculík was thrown out of the Communist party.

The least of the things that happened to him the following year was that he was readmitted to the party. In 1968 the writers, with Vaculík in the first rank, tried to force the pace of democratization, to rally the nation behind Alexander Dubček, and to prevent any attempt by the new party leadership to compromise with the pro-Soviet forces of conservatism. The "Two Thousand Word Manifesto," composed by Vaculík at the request of a group of scientists anxious that Dubček was losing impetus in the face of Soviet threats, was a blazing, reckless, and often comic argument against hesitation which led instantly to a major crisis. Leonid Brezhnev, no doubt assuming that the manifesto expressed the true feelings of the appalled Dubček, raged down the telephone and through the columns of *Pravda*. The Czechoslovak leadership temporarily lost its nerve in the face of a conservative counterattack and condemned the declaration. Thousands, including factory workers, nonetheless put their names to it.

It is probable that the "Two Thousand Word Manifesto" helped to convince the Soviet leaders that military intervention was necessary. Its very success in raising mass loyalty to Dubček to fresh heights horrified the Warsaw Pact regimes and increased the political isolation of Czechoslovakia. Many people would agree with William Shawcross that "the manifesto was a mistake, but it was probably inevitable" (William Shawcross, *Dubček* [London: George Weidenfeld & Nicolson Ltd., 1970]). Vaculík himself cannot be blamed for preferring not to discuss it these days.

Flung out of the party once more, Vaculík retreated after the invasion into silence and disgrace. Then, from the silence, there came this novel.

One could try to discuss *The Guinea Pigs* without bringing up Franz Kafka, but it would be a useless exercise. This is the same dim world of meaningless, menacing activity, broken into by strokes of atrocity delivered by an authority never named or identified. Vaculík certainly has Kafka on his mind; he said recently that "I don't want to go on living like a beetle who ceases to move and pretends to be dead because he's frightened of what's ahead." At the same time, as the Czech émigré satirist Gabriel Laub unpleasantly remarked, what was Kafkan fantasy when poor Franz was describing his metamorphosis into a cockroach has become mere reportage in contemporary Prague. The central personage of *The Guinea Pigs,* however, a little Prague bank clerk, belongs to another dynasty of characters in Czech literature: the fetidly possessive little house-tyrants who cuff their children, cringe to their masters, and go in for some anal collection-mania or other—stamps or preferably money.

The clerk works in a strange bank. He is servile there but also inquisitive. In this bank everybody pinches the money and tries to walk out with it, only to be searched by the security guards, who take most of their bank notes away again. The trouble is that there is a discrepancy between the amount confiscated by the guards and the amount returned to the bank, where the clerks spend their days putting all the bills together again in bundles of consecutive note-numbers. A fearsome anxiety grows at the idea that the missing notes are creating some secret, parallel circulation of their own: The economy, society itself, is threatened. Only one man has a theory of what is happening, an ancient employee who shrieks at a staff meeting that the "mysterious circulation" is the first turn of a whirlpool that will suck everything down with it: "the Maelstrom." In his smelly little room in the rafters of the bank this old man is himself up to something mysterious. The bank clerk knows that curiosity is dangerous, but he begins to spy on him.

At home the clerk begins to keep guinea pigs. They absorb his two young sons and worry his wife. The clerk, when nobody is looking, begins to play with them himself. He entertains them with his violin. He gives them intelligence tests and little feats to perform. He experiments and manipulates them; he measures their tiny fears and tiny turds. He puts them in danger, then in terror. He tortures them.

So the novel goes forward, to a hideous and bewildering conclusion. Vaculík has invented a world in which guinea pigs are human, like children and women, but men who go out of doors into that world are metamorphosed into creatures. Their last human trait to survive is inquisitiveness, and those who are too inquisitive disappear. There is no more horrible fable of alienation than this.

The Guinea Pigs is full of imagery and ominous symbols which operate at the surreal level. To stop and ask, What does the "secret circulation" stand for?, or What is it that is hidden in the ancient employee's barrel?, is to look for the wrong type of effect. I once asked Vaculík what the barrel (which looms rather large) did contain. He grinned at me under his black moustache and said that he didn't know—whatever I liked. This infuriated another Czech writer in the room, who said that Vaculík ought to know, even if he didn't tell the reader. The argument at least showed the extent to which Vaculík has diverged from the openness of most Czech writing, in the direction of the conspiratorial privacy that makes so much Polish fiction "difficult" and ambiguous.

Nor should this novel be taken too politically, as if it related only to the recent past of Czechoslovakia or deserved special consideration because of that context. "I cannot discuss my country's regime on the foreign book market," Vaculík told a German newspaper in 1972, "and I don't wish to. . . . He who feels impelled to write against the regime all the time is allowing himself to be prevented by the regime from writing about anything else. Also I feel it offensive when an outsider considers us to be an especially unfortunate people. We still belong to Europe; we have one of the European regimes that was once upon a time allocated to us."

Much earlier, he had said to Antonin J. Liehm, and this does have significance for *The Guinea Pigs*: "What power—what group—finds it eternally necessary to make people as characterless and submissive as possible? . . . Why must peoples' support be won only at the price of their moral devastation?"

NEAL ASCHERSON

xiii

The Guinea Pigs

I

There are more than a million people living in the city of Prague whom I'd just as soon not name here. Our family is originally from the country. Our family, that means me, my wife, and two tolerable little boys. The older boy isn't so little; he's thirteen, his name is Vašek, he is nearsighted and his eyes are brown. His interests are in construction projects, preferably where work is in progress and in passenger vehicles, preferably on rails, but also in the municipal underground network of canals containing water pipes, gas pipes, steam pipes, electrical and telephone cables and the like. Our Vašek is usually late for school because he usually winds up standing over some excavation, gazing into it much longer than we consider necessary. That is why Vašek likes weekdays. The younger boy is nine-year-old Pavel; he is nearsighted, has brown eyes and is interested in everything, preferably what Vašek is doing. Furthermore he is interested in construction projects, preferably where work is in progress, and passenger vehicles, preferably on rails. But the nature of his interest in these subjects is different from that of his brother. Let me give you an example.

When our boys ask to go outside, on a drizzly Sunday afternoon when you'd rather stay home, they will invariably take off for one of the railroad stations. They'll lollygag around on the platform for a while, but soon they'll run along the tracks toward the beautiful, rain and smoke enfolded roundhouse. Not daring to go inside, they'll stand around under the eaves of some dusty, sooty shed, lean against the outer wall, scraping their shoulder blades back and forth, and observe the traffic. When they finally arrive home, a little smarter than when they left, we bawl them out as if we had missed them; they have a snack, whereupon they retire to their room and engage in the following activities: Vašek immediately picks up where he left off in the construction of, say, a mobile crane for loading coal, while Pavel immediately takes some paper and begins to design a never-to-exist railway yard, with particular attention to the roundhouse turntable. Now that ought to tell you something about the difference in the nature of their interests in the same subjects. Perhaps I needn't elaborate, the brighter ones among my readers have already deduced that the lenses of Pavel's glasses are. thicker, and that he is chubbier.

So much for the boys, and now to us parents. Me, I am the Daddy. My name is Vašek and I work in an office at the State Bank. That is the fancy building on Wenceslas Square, all marble on the outside, but don't let that fool you about the inside. Maybe all I need tell you is that sometimes, on the days that we bank clerks (or "bankers") get to count out our salaries and tuck them in our billfolds, we keep casting uneasy glances towards the fancy revolving doors to our bank, afraid that someone might come in to withdraw his savings. And our salaries, for all that, aren't much to speak of, either. As the saying goes, barely enough to keep us from stealing. And for that matter, why not admit it, we do steal. But our efforts are desperate attempts, and only rarely does one of us succeed in bringing any stolen money home to his wife and children. There are guards at the bank exists and they search everyone carefully, confiscating everything that we don't have a receipt for, proving that we brought it into the bank that morning. But don't get the mistaken impression that what they confiscate gets put back in the treasury! At least, we the bankers of the State Bank, never see it there again. There are several varying opinions about it. And if, my dear young readers, you occasionally, frequently find yourselves wondering, along with your Mommies and your Daddies, why our national economy is in the state it is in, you might consider as part of the reply the facts that I have just inadvertently revealed to you. But this problem belongs in a mystery story rather than in a book about Nature, like this one. My wife, whom the boys, true to Nature, prefer to call Mom, is named Eva. She is a teacher, but there's no harm in that.

Our family comes from the country. Fifteen years ago, Eva and I moved to Prague with the intention of staying here for about five years—time enough to fulfill some of our patriotic needs with respect to the capital—and then removing ourselves and finding a place near our native towns for the best part of our lives. Sometimes, though, man departs from some of his intentions, while he follows alternate routes in the interest of maintaining his standard of living. And so we are still counting on returning to our native cemetery.

What bothers a country person living in Prague, for the most part, is the hostility of the people and the lack of the proximity of Nature. Stronger individuals, on the other hand, don't devote themselves much to being bothered and soon discover freedoms that they would never have had in the country. But a man like that keeps on bragging about being a country boy at heart, because in Prague—a city that has yet to learn to behave in every sense like a metropolis—it speaks for him rather than against him. But Nature, that is something that all of us country people in Prague miss the most.

Every spring, we take our boys across Levý Hradec to the towering hilltop Řivnáč, where the pasqueflower blossoms in profusion. Towering, my dear young readers, means that it towers, that it is tall and magnificent. At cherry time, our excursions almost always include a compulsory trip to the rocky Kozí hřbety cliffs beyond Suchdol. Compulsory means we have to, but it isn't too bad at cherry time, on account of the cherries.

When we go on these hikes together, we have to be a little considerate of each other. A trip to the Botanical Gardens is, for people like Eva and myself, a concentrated afternoon of pleasant enlightenment for middle-aged dullards who in the course of five years have yet to fix in their minds which chervil it is that goes by the name of *Anthriscus pers.*, whereas for their children Vašek and Pavel, it is sheer boredom. Enlightenment means learning. But they like going there with us anyway. In exchange, we like going with them to the Hlubočepy Valley, where the viaducts bearing two railroads intertwine in a mind-boggling view for our two boys. Meanwhile the two of us adults are more taken by the sight of the poor little cottages that remain as vestiges of the gone-by days when people led more neighborly lives; the cottages are kept in such good repair that it is touching. Under the old stone viaducts, the cottages rest by the banks of the brook, with stone stairs leading down to the water, and they are a truly picturesque sight. Picturesque must mean pretty like a picture, and what mind-boggling is, I'm not sure.

But as for you, my dear young readers, perhaps freshly transplanted to Prague by your parents—get ready for the fact that a stroll through Nature here will often be a mournful occasion. In Prague and its environs, smack under the nose of the Minister of Agriculture, you can find the largest number of arid and badly worked fields that I have ever seen. It is as if grass, trees and water have no value at all. And water to swim in—pleasant, clean swimming water is something that you'll have as much trouble finding as we did. One summer we discovered two little lakes in Sedlec, right near the Vltava Embankment. The Embankment, children, is a stone wall, with heavy iron rings where they can tie boats that come from Austria. Austria is—but let's leave that for some other time. The lakes, with reeds growing all around, were rectangular in shape, they had sandy bottoms and shallow water, just what we were looking for. They probably were created when they were bulldozing sand. Bulldozing means working with a bulldozer. But we only went swimming there about three times because we couldn't get used to the view of the river flowing past beyond the dike: it was full of lazily floating feces and rubber contraceptives.

4

But let's not talk about filth, children, let's talk about pets, which are nicer. We never seriously had any pets at home. Keeping a dog in Prague is something of a luxury, keeping a cat is difficult. We did try it with a tom-kitten once, that's a baby tomcat. He was cute and charming and amusing. Yes, the kitten was fun and the boys were naughty, but he scratched up all our furniture and things, and ended up peeing in the shoe-rack, so we got rid of him. "Got rid of him" is a very suspect turn of phrase that I never used to like; it could mean giving him away, selling him, banishing him, but it could also mean drowning him, feeding him to a larger animal, smashing his head against a wall or even worse. When I say "got rid of him," it only means that we gave him away, nothing worse than that.

On Saturday I made a little bed for the soot-black kitten in the bottom of a wicker basket, Eva sewed a canvas top onto the basket, and I took off to visit a friend of ours who lives in the woods. On my way there, I saved the life of a viper that I saw from a bridge I was crossing. It was struggling to get out of the forest creek, under the overhanging bank. A viper, children, is a poisonous snake. I happened to see it because I had stopped on the bridge, partly to rest for a moment, and partly because that would have been a perfect chance to drown the kitchen, if that had been my intention. It was with a feeling of horror that I imagined how I would feel if I were sewed up in a basket and the water started to seep in, and me not able to get out. I also wondered what they would say at the State Bank. And that was when I caught sight of the snake in the water.

I knew right away that it wasn't a harmless water snake. The common water snake would behave far more skillfully in the water, and besides, the writhing snake under the bridge had the typical zigzag pattern of a viper down its back. The poor thing was apparently fighting with all that was left of its feeble strength. It was so exhausted that it couldn't even turn itself around so that it might pursue a cross current direction towards the other side, where the bank had a gentler slope to it and where it could have easily wiggled out of the water. Instead, it writhed at the base of the other, steeper bank, bumping its head into the soil under the overhanging ledge, making pieces of the bank break off and float on downstream. First, of course, I asked myself whether or not a viper deserves saving. My first impulse was to hit it on the head with a rock. After I had saved it and it had disappeared into the underbrush, I realized that I didn't have the children with me, and that if I had wanted to, I could have sat by the creek as long as I pleased, watching to see what it would do, how it would approach the end of its life, and possibly rescuing it at the last possible instant.

If it seems to you, my dear young readers, that my thinking was a bit perverted, let me disclose to you a minor truth—but consider it a small lesson of a moral nature—all things being equal, my purest and most natural instinct was when I wanted to kill the snake. And my most perverted impulse, if you will, was—having saved its life already—my present urge to dissect the act for you here, and your being so interested in it. If I were truly noble, I'd have helped the viper out of the water and walked away without ever a second thought, and above all without writing about it here, possibly without writing anything about anything ever again. You see, I have my own theory about virtue. It came to me one day when I was in the woodshed chopping kindling when I was fourteen. It is such a good theory that I wouldn't change a word of it even now that I'm almost forty and on the verge of early old age. I might add that if any of you hasn't come up with his own original theory about at least one thing in life before you turn fifteen, you'll never come up with one later, not about anything, even if you get to be a member of the Academy of Arts and Sciences. But back to the viper.

I thought about fishing it out of the water with my bare hands, but I wasn't quite sure that it was in such a bad state that it would not to bite me. So instead, I found myself a forked stick, but the snake didn't want to let me pick it up on the branch, or to change its direction, either. It kept squirming away and banging its head against the bank. Its lack of comprehension annoyed me to the point of evoking the urge to whack it across the skull with my stick. I stifled the impulse, and instead found myself another branch, this one with a lot of tiny dense twigs on the end, and then I pushed and shoved the little reptile all the way to the shallows on the other side. It crept weakly up out of the hostile element and aimed without delay for the underbrush in a stiff crawl. I was sorry that my children hadn't been in on it. How often do we have the opportunity to treat an opponent with such obvious magnanimity?

But those of my young readers with a good memory must be on the verge of reminding me that I've drifted away from the subject of the kitten in the basket. Well, anyway, it was a slightly foggy spring day, and the kitten was travelling through the wood in a basket. When we reached a broad place in the path, out of sheer excess energy, I took and swung the basket around a few times over my head and down again. Of course I was careful that the velocity (that is, the speed) was not too small for the kitten, because, if the revolutions had been too slow, the kitten would have bounced around inside the basket for lack of gravity. I didn't want him to hurt himself, and so I was considerate enough to keep increasing the speed of rotation, until my shoulder began to ache. But I don't think any of you would have done any less.

The kitten was welcomed warmly at my friend's home. It got some milk and some meat. I got some soup from the lady of the house, and some meat, some strawberry pudding and some coffee. Yum. The house was in the woods, and the doors and the windows were open all the livelong day. The kitten could come and go as he pleased, and didn't have to explain anything to anybody. Nobody even asked him about anything. Right at the foot of the forest was a village, certainly full of mice, with probably even a few cats. As I sat there eating my strawberry pudding and drinking my coffee, I looked out the door and the windows to assess the kitten's new possibilities, and I wished that I could have something like that too. I told the lady, and she laughed. But it never came true, and it isn't going to, because, children dear, a bank is, after all, a bank.

I saw our kitten once more after that, and that was the last time Vašek and Pavel saw him too. We drove out to see my friends and pick a few blackberries. The tom-kitten had become a tomcat by then, and didn't recognize us at all. When we arrived, he crept under the bed and kept giving us hostile looks. They told us that he didn't play with anyone any more, and that we were lucky to have even found him at home, because most of the time he was out gallivanting like some telephone linesman. And sure enough, we hadn't been sitting there for more than ten minutes when the cat took advantage of our having turned our attention to some raspberry pudding, and without a word, jumped up on the window sill with his bag of tools, and that was that. Later on we heard that he had begun coming home from his trips at longer and longer intervals, and that his tool chest was getting heavier too. He had become accustomed to a life of danger, he didn't want to live any other way. If it cost him his life, nobody is going to hold an investigation or bear him any ill will, only a few cats will bear a few litters of young ones more or less for a while after he is gone.

But Eva and I don't want any more young ones; two boys like Vašek and Pavel are plenty, our world being what it is.

II

The kitten had only spent a few weeks with us, but it had made a permanent mark on our family—partly on the shoe rack, and partly on the minds of our boys. They grieved, they reminisced, they debated about cats; all of a sudden they saw cats everywhere. They made a special trip to the zoo to see a wildcat. Whenever I came home from the bank in a bad mood, they would say that I'm grouchy as an old tomcat that doesn't know how to play any more. Vašek made friends with a boy whose family was known for the fact that they had a houseful of cats. When we didn't let him bring home a kitten from their house, he at least began bringing home some fleas. As for Pavel, he just sat around drawing pictures of cats. He got to be so good at it that you could tell their moods and states of mind from the looks on their pencilled faces. One day he offered to give me a picture showing an old, weary tomcat in a stance that for all the world recalled a well-known bank clerk just returning from his State Bank, standing in the doorway hollering, "Where the devil is that Vašek again? Out at the excavations again, I bet!"

Country people that we were, Eva and I became increasingly

9

aware of the fact that without the company of animals, a human's life just isn't right. In addition, Eva came up with an explanation of why you school children nowadays are so cruel to your friends and to trees. A city person's love for Nature, says Eva, is a reflection of old recollections. Partly, it reflects his memory of his own personal, individual childhood, and partly—vaguely and more or less subconsciously—an atavistic kind of memory of the youth of the city when it was still a village. Rural life renews and refreshes the emotions of city people. But all that will soon become extinct, Eva maintains, because today even the fields have been turned into potato factories and the cows are being transformed into machines for the production of milk. Long ago, when one person out of two had at least a cow or a horse to look after, sometimes the whole population would have cows and horses on its mind. It is a fact that love of these animals was born of their usefulness, but that's not what counts today, says Eva. Unfortunately, nowadays the few milk cows that live in the cow stalls in the Republic's dairy farm cooperatives can't account for all of Czechoslovakia's emotions towards cows.

I think my Eva is largely right. Largely, I say, but—as usual— she's not entirely right. Her utilitarian explanation, dear children, is not enough for you or for me. Of course, we agree with Eva that the usefulness of those beasts is a *conditio sine qua non,* but aside from that, one's emotional relationship to them has an explanation that is profoundly psychological. I will endeavor to make an *ex abrupto* outline for you, even though it all is somewhat marginal to the simple tale about animals that I have been working towards since I started.

As you know, a man can be a prince or the merest of the prince's non-devoted slaves. In a modern state he can be the President or the merest of his non-voters. There is no reason to go into detail as to which of these he is more likely to be. The position of a poor sap like that, at the bottom stratum of the social structure, is typified by his absolute helplessness. The one at the bottom is unhappy because he has to obey everybody, and there is no one to obey him. But if he finds that he has at least one creature even lower than himself, the world takes on an

10

entirely different aspect. Social structures expand, and the bottom stratum retreats by a horse's length, by the height of a cow, by the breadth of a dog. Once we give him a dog of his own, a fellow who has felt like a dog all day has someone he can order around, and someone he can kick around, too. And because he could even kill him if he wanted to, he will be all the more careful of him. True, he may really kick him once in a while . . . but then he'll suddenly feel sorry for him. Sorry! And thus pity is born. Sympathy. You poor little beast, you're just as badly off as I am, come to daddy, poor little thing! A little girl denies her budding cruelty at the sight of the fluffy goslings placed in her care, only to give vent—whip of willow branch in hand—to her budding gentleness. And from then on, she will find both those attributes within herself, although—fortunately for us—she will prefer to make use of the latter one.

So while Eva's idea of "the peasant and his cow" is that the peasant loves his cow because she feeds him, let me advise you, boys and girls, to learn to view that twosome from another angle as well: The peasant is fond of his cow because he feeds her even though he could, if he so desired, break her back with a club. That is a psychological explanation *par excellence*.

So that the kitten showed our children that there is something else in the world besides railroads and vehicles, preferably for passenger transport. The kitten aroused something in them, and then he left them. But what's to be done? Try a dog? Eva and I agreed that if we had a house like the ones we saw under the viaduct in suburban Hlubočepy, we could have both a dog and a cat. And even chickens, maybe.

"Wouldn't you like to have a cow?" I teased her.

"If I had a cow and chickens, I'd have to have a garden, and at least a piece of field like my folks used to have, but then I'd quit teaching right away," she declared.

"And if we had that kind of thing," I said, "I'd manage it conscientiously, efficiently and with foresight, and we'd never put the money we'd earn into any State Bank."

But all that was just meaningless talk, the way big people often do. Eva could never leave her school, the only thing that could happen is that they could throw her out, and me too. The hardest thing in the world, girls and boys, is to change your lives of your own free will. Even if you are absolutely convinced that you're the engineer on your own locomotive, someone else is always going to flip the switch that makes you change tracks, and it's usually somebody who knows much less than you do.

There's a fellow at the bank where I work, my colleague, his name is Mr. Karásek, and some time ago, he had told me that they have guinea pigs at home. It was late in the day, Karásek had just changed into his street shoes under his desk, and was slipping into his jacket over by the wardrobe, when he gave a sigh of relief.

"I must say, it'll be nice to get home again."

"What's there so interesting at home?" it occurred to me to ask, because I knew that his children were grown and gone.

"Guinea pigs," he said, "a pair of guinea pigs, that's all."

We had never brought it up since, because I hadn't been interested. Now I remembered the guinea pigs. Right away, I asked Karásek what they eat and what they need in general. I found out that the Peruvian Guinea Pig (*Cavia porcellus*) is a very undemanding creature as to fodder and space—that it's a rodent, that it lives on grain, vegetables and grass, a little hay in the winter, and when there isn't any grain, then oatmeal. But one thing is that we have to wash the vegetables thoroughly, particularly the lettuce, so the guinea pig wouldn't eat any of the sprays and fertilizers they use. The Peruvian Guinea Pig (*Cavia porcellus*, as I mentioned before) lives in a box big enough for him to run around in. He is a mild-tempered animal, with clean habits. He likes the shade. He doesn't drink any fluids at all, don't give him any! Most frequent causes of death are pneumonia and some form of diarrhea. What else? . . . They are simply charming animals. Karásek's *Cavia porcellus* (Peruvian Guinea Pig) ostensibly climbs onto the palm of Mr. Karásek's hand, and then shinnies up his arm to his shoulder. He will sit there for maybe half an hour on Mr. Karásek's shoulder gazing down on sheets of paper with numbers on them. The male treats the female very tenderly. A guinea pig that lives alone is supposed to be lazy and

12

depressed to the point of utter stupidity. I asked Karásek whether he didn't mind at first that the guinea pig looks like a big rat. He replied with astonishment that it doesn't look like a rat at all, but rather like a little bunny rabbit. There is not much by way of information that can surprise a fellow today, and there is still less than can please him as much as that last bit of information pleased me.

Christmas was coming, and we were trying to get presents together. I thought of a guinea pig. I discussed it with Eva, wondering if it wouldn't be just the gift for our boys, a cure for Pavel's yearning and for Vašek's fleas as well. Eva rejected the idea of a guinea pig most resolutely; she said that they made her sick, and so the very next day I set out to buy a guinea pig. It was early on the morning of Christmas Eve. There were any number of guinea pigs at the store, all different colors. I picked a white one with red eyes. It was little, but not the littlest of all. I wouldn't have liked tearing the smallest guinea pig they had out of its family circle. Besides, it might up and die on us. I did want a young guinea pig, though, because I wanted it to get used to Pavel as it grew up, and also, so that we all could watch and observe its development through its entire life-cycle. I bought some feed for it too, some sort of a mixture of rye and all sorts of seed.

They had all kinds of things in that store. I mean, besides tropical fish and birds, they had turtles and hamsters. They even had a weasel there, exceptionally. I thought to myself that if they sold it to someone, they would have a steady customer for guinea pigs. The weasel was pacing its wire cage like a little demon. I asked what it was, and they said it was a weasel. There was a store full of customers, mainly for fish and birds. I wondered what anyone would want with a turtle that barely budges. I found the hamsters nasty, with their nervous hopping around and their quivering snuffling. I even thought they stank. A guinea pig is better. I was surprised that it only cost fourteen crowns.

In the trolley car, the guinea pig's bottom warmed up his box, and the box in turn warmed up my palm. I was sure that very few of the people in the trolley car were hurrying home with such a clever present at such a last moment. Eva wasn't angry. The warm box frightened her a little, but when she tipped open the lid and the two little red eyes flashed like two rubies on a white fur coat, she was pleasantly surprised and moved.

"Where is his tail?" she asked.

"Doesn't have a tail," I replied.

"How come? I thought that a guinea pig was like a rat."

"I knew that was what you thought," I laughed.

"You're going to have to come and kill the carp for me," she said, and I stopped laughing abruptly.

Christmas that year was the Christmas that we will always refer to as the Christmas with the Guinea Pig.

What a present!

It had all the attributes of a good gift: first of all, it came as a complete surprise; secondly, it fulfilled some kind of a big wish, and besides, it was beautiful and touching, and then it was simple, and finally, it was even rare. To think of a present like that, a person would first of all have to be really clever and observant; then, he would have to be quick; furthermore, he would have to have a feeling for the rarity of the moment: to know the desire of the recipient, to have a certain feeling towards him and know how to estimate the response. He would have to possess good taste combined with a sense of humor, be profound, because he had racked his brain until he came up with it, but he would have to know how to stand firm, not to let other people dissuade him. Nor could he be too lazy to go out of his way, nor too stingy to regret the money. And in the twelfth place, he would also have to be a considerate person, not to have bought the weasel.

And Pavel!

According to our family tradition, Pavel, as the youngest, distributes the packages and the rest of us sit around quietly. Quietly. When he picked up the box and read his name, he stopped cold and couldn't go on. He weighed the shifting mass inside the box, and you could see by the look on his face that his imagination had begun to function. He had to unwrap his present right away. . . .

14

"Gee, it's great, look, folks, look what I got, what is it? Something with little red eyes, Mom! Vašek! Dad! And I got some turds, too, look!"

He laughed, ran around the room, surprised, pleased, shaking his head.

"Did you ever get anything like that? I mean when you were kids?"

"It's a guinea pig," said mother, and gave me a joyful look.

Pavel flew around the room again and returned to the box on the floor. The guinea pig was sitting in it, tremulously squeezed in the corner of its temporary home, afraid even to wink an eye. Then all of a sudden it gave a feeble squeak, and it winked, and it surprised us all. But that wasn't the end of it. It began to turn around in spasms, scratching with its claws and squeaking louder and louder. Its thin voice sounded a little like the tin whistle that we call a nightingale. It was calling for someone, and we were all upset because we didn't know what to do. I told Pavel to close the lid in the meantime, and we continued with Christmas.

But anything that followed was anticlimactic. Vašek's present was pretty clever too; Eva had dug it up someplace: it was a construction set for a miniature scaffolding, like the kind they use to finish and repair the facades of buildings. Both boys were surprised and pleased, but they kept returning to the box with the live present, and wanting to play with it. However, it wasn't until they had put away all the books, shirts, papers and ribbons that they could take another look at the guinea pig, but they weren't allowed to squeeze it. Then we moved the little creature into a wooden margarine case with wood shavings at the bottom, because it was bigger; we poured some feed in a flowerpot dish, and Pavel brought a carrot from the pantry, having scrubbed it good and proper so the poor little thing shouldn't get sick his first day. But the guinea pig didn't eat a thing as long as we were watching, and when anyone wanted to pet it on the head, it would push his finger away with a resolute and surprisingly strong push of its head. Only after Vašek and Pavel had climbed into bed and turned off the light did it begin to wriggle and squirm in its box, rustle around, and then you could hear some tiny, sharp crunching. Pavel ran in to tell us about it, when Eva

15

and I were in bed, the lights out, and with entirely different things on our minds.

"All right, all right," I said, "but will the two of you get to sleep finally, damn it?"

During the night, I woke up for some unknown reason and realized that for two days I wouldn't have to go to the State Bank. I went out of the bedroom to get a drink of water and then I remembered something else that was nice—that we had a guinea pig. I slipped into the boys' room and turned on the light. The boys were sleeping like logs, the guinea pig was sitting in the corner of its box, burning through the shadows with its two little rubies.

III

The year was drawing to a close. Taking inventory in a bank is naturally different from stocktaking in, say, a bookshop. You can't stop the current circulation of currency, and pile it up and count it. So a bank inventory verges on the . . . on the indescribable.

It would be the right thing to do if everyone who takes money home with him—that is, steals it—were to be fired at the very least, or—the way they used to do in the First Republic or under the Austrian Empire—even put in jail. But they don't quite dare do that nowadays. We have a very strong trade union, because everybody belongs to it. There was once some talk about the possibility of setting up another one. If there were two unions, they wouldn't be so impossibly strong. But the talk was strictly unofficial. Unofficial talk, loved ones, means when people get together to exchange opinions by the tobacco shop and newsstand. One day an elderly banker let himself be heard voicing this opinion a short distance away from the newsstand, and they arrested him. It was the only time anyone was arrested, but it only depleted the ranks of thieves by a total of one, so it didn't help much.

17

It's no fun taking money out of the bank over and above your salary, because the probability that you'll get home with it is very small. But when out of sheer desperation we give up stealing every so often, the word always gets around the bank that so-and-so got away with a nice round sum. A report like that always inspires us to new attempts which always run up against the suddenly revitalized vigilance of the guards. And who is it that benefits from that?

There is an elderly gentleman working at our bank, a commercial engineer by the name of Chlebeček. He should have retired a long time ago, but the bank won't let him go because he is the last banker who still knows how to work with the system of *lombard* finance. Not that we use the lombard system in our finances—it is something that is used exclusively in capitalist credit operations so that we needn't really be interested in it at all. The good man's position in the bank is assured, however, because occasionally someone from the Ministry of Finance submits an enquiry about what lombard is. As for me, dear children, I don't know what lombard is.

One day this Mr. Chlebeček, who until then had remained largely unnoticed, sat down at a sheet of graph paper and set up a balance sheet that he kept up regularly over a period of several months. The results upset the entire State Bank. It had already been a matter of common knowledge that the money confiscated by the guards in their searches did not reappear in the treasury the next day. What Mr. Chlebeček, the elderly commercial engineer discovered was that this money never returns to the bank at all, not even through the market, not even through normal circulation of currency. Now any of you, dear hearts, who will ever have anything to do with trade or commerce must already be filled with justified astonishment, as future experts in the field of finance, an astonishment with underlying evil forebodings. . . . If this money were to be put through the mill and destroyed, we might think that it is a movingly simple and morally pure anti-inflationary measure organized by the usually ill-informed circles outside the sphere of economics. But since that is not the case, we are unable to make that assumption. Still, be that as it may, one thing remains certain, the amount of currency in circulation is dropping, not just relatively but absolutely. When it drops beyond a certain limit, the ratio between bank notes and bankers will drop below the permissible level and our bank will have to start laying off employees. That is the prognosis of our commercial engineer, Mr. Chlebeček, and that is our New Year's greeting for the forthcoming year.

But, dear hearts, let's not talk about the bank, let's talk about pets; they are nicer and more relaxing, too. I am lying on the floor, observing a guinea pig. Long-term observation puts me in a long-forgotten frame of mind. When was the last time I had observed anything? When I was little, in the meadow. I mean observation as a spiritual state.

Our day to day existence nowadays is by nature active. As individuals our lives consist of pressure. The life of society in sum—working, praying, enjoying itself—is imbued with aggressiveness; recognized, cultivated, accepted aggressiveness that is taken into account in all planning, not to mention production and diplomacy; and I even consider prayer to be an act of aggression with respect to God. The plan that has been implanted and instilled in us has aims that in the final analysis turn out to consist of—satisfaction. That is the target toward which our movements converge, even on Sundays, and even in our dreams. We consider a halt in our activity to be a postponement of satisfaction. Everything that happens, the broad current and cadence of events, even when it is pleasant and calm, must truthfully be read as a collision of cultivated aggressions. No one just sits around and waits for anything, because nothing comes to him who waits, and no one sits around and observes either. Observation is neither cultivated nor bred, no one instills it or implants it in anyone and it has been unconsciously renounced by one and all. Maybe the aged fall into it, unwittingly, when they are not reminiscing or meditating, or when they are not dozing or, perhaps, imperceptibly dead. True, we do have special observation laboratories and research agencies. But there, observation merely plays a role within the production or investment process, with some specific utilitarian aim. But that has nothing to do with the kind of observation that I am talking about.

True observation, as I have vaguely described it above, is a state of mind. Or it might be better defined as a manner of existence—one that is persevering, shall we say passive, silent, contemplative. Waiting? No, not waiting, waiting for what? An observer does not experience the passage of time, he isn't a farmer impatient for his seeds to germinate. A true observer has no interest in the outcome of his observation, he isn't a cat observing the behavior of a mouse. The kind of observation that I have in mind is a state of the body that in no way disturbs the state of mind that is. The mind, or spirit, shall I say, is preoccupied, but not tense with expectation. It is neither enthused nor disenchanted, because it does not pass judgment. Observation has something to do with self-forgetfulness. So that it follows that it is something that only man, of all creatures, is capable of producing; and yet it requires that he relinquish all human interest in the phenomenon under observation. God would be an exemplary observer. The eyes of an ideal observer would have no connections to his paws whereby he might intervene in the process being observed. Only God does not help or hinder anything—as if he were watching without seeing, or else seeing, with all his stocks in another corporation.

But, my dears, let us not even talk of God, but rather about pets, they are smaller and clearer. I took a wooden box of foreign make and made a cage for the guinea pig. Instead of a front wall, the cage had a wire mesh the height of the span of a child's hand. In order to allow the guinea pig to feel safe from beasts of prey—though we don't harbor any in our house—the cage was equipped with a lid. But that wasn't enough for Pavel, and he too put a little box from a toy car in the cage. The guinea pig threw himself into it head first as if it were a cozy burrow. With considerable effort, so that its fur got all mussed up, it turned over in it till it was right side up, and then it settled down contentedly. Resting its chin on its front paws like an old lady tobacconist, mustache and all, it sat there staring out.

Now it has all the privacy it wants, when it wants it. When it isn't walking around the cage, it sits in its box and slowly nibbles at it; one of these days it is going to eat it up completely. One might say that as a rodent, it has its voracious side.

We were afraid, at the start, that Pavel would drag the guinea pig bedraggled. But even though he is forever doing something for it, he is pretty much aware of the difference between the needs of a four-week-old guinea pig and a nine-year-old boy. The guinea pig is pretty fortunate not to have gotten into the hands of one of you other children or, what would be even worse, one of you little girls. Little girls are the worst things there are nowadays. They don't have anything to do, they have practically nothing to worry about all day, and so when they want to take care of somebody, they can do more harm than good, thanks to their obtuse mothers. Obtuse means broad, when talking of angles, but when it comes to mothers, obtuse means decorative, lazy and common. You might as well know it, little girls, I am fed up to here with those mothers of yours. I'm concerned about which of you, you giggling little know-nothings—not even how to play the silly piano—which of you are the ones our boys are going to marry. A kick down the stairs, that's what we'll give you. All right. Relax, light up your future cigarette and hear me out now, before it's too late: I can well imagine what would have happened if the guinea pig had been given to one of you little girls of the age of Pavel instead of to him. You would cuddle it, you little silly ones, you'd squeeze it and pet it and snuggle it until, out of sheer ecstasy, it would quit eating, its fur would get all raunchy, its eyes would fade and finally they would go out completely. We know what would happen next: you would take it and, tearfully, mournfully, with a pleasant feeling of grief, you would bury it and be forever carrying flowers to its grave.

On the other hand, Pavel's attentions are responsible. He sees to it that the guinea pig has enough privacy. He cleans its cage and moistens its grain. He too might get it into his head that the guinea pig's fur is dirty and that it needs a bath. But he knows that a guinea pig isn't allowed to get in the water, because that might kill it. It took Pavel a long time to figure out when a guinea pig sleeps, and he was really worried about whether it really got enough sleep at our house. The only way we ever saw it sleeping was sitting up, with its eyes half open. When one day Pavel finally found it lying on its side like a real pig, he ran to announce it to us, having deduced that Albínek had apparently begun to get used to us.

"He feels at home now," said Pavel.

"He can't feel at home, he hasn't got a house," said Vašek.

"A home doesn't necessarily mean a house," said the teacher.

"And home is where the house is," I said.

And so Vašek set up his miniature scaffolding all around Albínek's cage, as if it were an apartment house whose facade needed repairs. He took a round tin box, put it on an axle and connected it to an electric motor to make a cement mixer. Then he made himself a trowel and some buckets and things; he attached a pulley to the scaffolding and proceeded to raise the concrete to the proper heights.

Every morning when Vašek goes off to school, two bricklayers, Mr. Kalfas and Mr. Malvaz, climb the ladders and levels of the scaffolding and go to work. After school, Vašek always hurries home in order to catch them before quitting time. They are still there, Mr. Kalfas and Mr. Malvaz; they're just on their coffee break, drinking beer and smoking cigarettes. The house took an incredibly short time to build, something in the area of about two weeks. Then Vašek told Pavel, "Now you finally have a house for that Albínek of yours." And he took down the scaffolding.

"Thank you, Mr. Kalfas, thank you Mr. Malvaz, thank you Vašek," said Pavel gravely.

"Mr. Vašek," said the foreman.

We expected Albínek to try to get out of his cage, and we were afraid we'd forever be stepping on him. But a guinea pig isn't a kitten. A guinea pig is not an inquisitive creature; it sees no reason to change its geographical location. On the contrary, whenever we take him out of his cage, he is unhappy and keeps on squealing. He learned to climb over the wire mesh. At first he was clumsy about it, getting his claws entangled in the loops, but now he knows how to push himself off, jump up on the edge, and fall over on the other side. But the only direction in which he ever climbs it is to get in, it would never occur to him to try to climb out!

He doesn't do anything. I don't know how come Karásek's guinea pig climbs on his palm. Why? Because when I stand our guinea pig on the floor, he always moves away from us, never towards us. And he skitters along the wall, like a mouse. The only times he behaves a bit more freely is when he is in his cage, where he feels secure. There, he even displays certain lukewarm social inclinations. He will shuffle over to a hand near the mesh, but only when he is hungry. When you scratch the back of his neck, he will stand still and half close his eyes. But when you pet him on the head, he will push your finger away with some sort of irate instinct. And what he can't stand at all is a touch near his behind. That makes him run away, and if he can't, he squeals frantically, and turns to the hand that is annoying him with an irate clatter of his teeth; I know for a fact that if he were big enough, say, up to my knees, he would bite off your hand. *Your* hand, because I would know better than to tease him. His teeth, those two big incisors on top and the two below, are forever clattering, no matter what the subject. But he never bites anyone. At first we thought that a guinea pig wouldn't even have the strength to bite through a finger. But we found out differently one day when Eva was handing him a carrot, and—entirely by accident, mind you—he grabbed her finger out of sheer impatience. A guinea pig has plenty of strength in its teeth. Our logic led us to the deduction that what happened to Pavel's nose was that it got bitten, and not that he scratched himself the way he said.

I like to lie on the floor and gaze into the cage. The guinea pig usually sits for a while, waiting to see what my presence will mean in his life. Then he moves, carefully, and when he sees that nothing disastrous has happened, he takes a few shuffling steps. In a little while, he has forgotten about me. Now and then he picks up a blade of grass and works at it diligently. Then he goes on, mumbling under his breath, dropping a turd now and then. A tiny dry turd, the kind that had begun to materialize in Pavel's bed, until we considered taking Pavel to the doctor. I like it when Albínek sits up on his little butt and cleans his face with his front legs, snuffling softly all the while. Or, sometimes he itches, and so he lies down on his side and scratches behind his ear with his hind leg. I think that he is happy with us, and that he has even put on a little weight.

There are times when I wonder what it is. A furry machine? An idea of God's that went astray for want of an education, having come up against an obstacle? Who is responsible for that little bundle? It knows how to walk, it has a call of sorts, it watches, it breathes. But all the same, I'm not possessed of the desire of little boys in the best of years: to see how it works. The floor is flat and warm. When I pick the little creature up, it jerks around in the air, it tries to defend itself by scratching with its harmless claws, and then it goes limp like a warm sack containing a complete set of little innards. Strange, strange. I place the guinea pig on my hand, it turns round on it, sniffing, leaning over the edge into the pit below, but it stays there, it knows. There is only one direction in which it can go, and it discovers it: up the arm, into the sleeve. Whoops, and there it goes, nosing its way deeper and deeper. It's awfully nice.

I can't seem to get adjusted to the fact that they sell it. I mean, that they're allowed to. They might just as well sell me to a guinea pig. Decisions! A person can buy one animal after another, and no one even bothers to ask, where do you put them all? Put them? The beast was quarrelsome, offensive, vain, sassy, I got rid of it. A horse, hundreds of times larger and more, isn't any better off. Not buying slaves is a matter of habit. Terror applies to everyone; don't nail frogs to wooden gates, little boys, or women to tables, troops! Mr. Chlebeček is exceptionally ugly to look at. Runny popeyes, a weepy red nose, rotten teeth. And his feet stink. The little guinea pig's fur is as sweet and fragrant as a baby kid's. Replacing it in its cage, I am shaken. It's only been with us for a few days and already it thinks that it has its home, its residential right, its intimacy, its sovereignty and its freedom

24

of the press. When they release it from a dangerous situation and it arrives home, it goes and takes a leak, straightens its tie, cleans its face, it even goes to work on its toenails, nibbling away audibly on its long claws. It climbs into its box, turns around with effort and places its little face on its hands, stares and breathes, its eyes begin to close. Sunday afternoon. Eva is asleep too; she fell asleep reading the Literary News; she doesn't have the slightest awareness of the newspaper, or of the grum little girl that is one of her pupils in school. The boys are off at the railroad station. No homework for them! I ought to take a look at Pavel's Pupil's Report Book when I get up off the floor. But I can't do it. I can't seem to establish the connections to my paws.

When I finally succeeded in putting my paws into operation, I started digging in Pavel's school bag. His Pupil's Report Book wasn't there, but I found plenty of interesting reading there all the same. There wasn't anything about guinea pigs, though. I was astonished at such a gross omission and proceeded to write an article for the third grade reader. Here it is:

"The Guinea Pig. We have a guinea pig at home. Our guinea pig is small and sweet. It has white fur and red eyes. Its name is Albínek. Albínek sits, breathes and watches. It sits and watches all day. It sits and watches and eats vegetables, rye and hay. It makes lots of little black turds. Pavel looks and cries, 'Look, Albi, look! Look what you did!'

Vašek cries, 'That's all right, he is just a little guinea pig!'

Mother cries, 'He is just a little guinea pig, and he has to eat!'

Father cries, 'Whoever eats, potties.'

We all love Albínek."

When I finished writing the article, I sent it to Ministry of Education, Reader Department, Fourth Grade Division. I can't wait to see Pavel's face when his classroom teacher gives him next year's reader.

IV

Two weeks later I got the article about the guinea pig back from the Ministry of Education. In the enclosed letter of rejection, the yellow funks wrote me that they couldn't include it in the reader because it's too long. They can't fool me, that's what every editor says when he doesn't feel like printing the truth, particularly when it is obvious even to a nine-year-old. Too long. Too long! At first I wanted to go to that ministry of theirs, then I decided it would be enough to write them a letter, and then I decided to forget it—what's the use of debasing myself?

For that matter, what's the difference? Why write someplace, and then, why write articles about a guinea pig that is perfectly all right? Just looking at it, I can tell right off what is really important. If a person is at odds with his life, he'll pine away out of sheer senseless ambition, foolish jeolousy and base envy. A normal person doesn't write any place. Either he is all right, in bank and bladder, or he isn't, but if at least his brain is all right, he is perfectly aware of the fact that no one is going to set him all right besides himself. Maybe a few people can sponge off his misery before they finally just drop him the way he is. So why write? Sleeping is better. Writing is always some sort of expression of helplessness or the product of a case of messed-up nerves, disclosing complexes or a bad conscience. The greater the literature, the greater the hysteria, really; think it over. *Silent Flows the Don*, is it a bad conscience for the ones that were killed, or an inferiority complex reflecting a dearth of dead when the season was so promising? Writing is healthy only when it is a pastime, a hobby, recreation for the writer or the reader, or a livelihood. I, for example, I am enjoying myself and avoiding doing my calculations.

But the other day when I couldn't answer offhand how much nine times seventeen is, that really surprised me. I was walking Eva to work, and as we approached her school, there was a tangle of little girls and bigger girls milling around. All of a sudden, one little figure pulled away from the bunch and ran out to meet us, her arms spread wide. She ran a little clumsily, as if one foot were tripping over the other, but even from a distance you could see the smile on her face. I thought that it was one of Eva's pupils running to meet her favorite teacher, and Eva looked that way too. But when the little girl stumbled up to us, she threw herself at me, wound her arms around my waist, raised her face and grinned. Eva and I were both astonished, and the only way I can explain it is that the child had in fact started running towards her teacher, and when she was halfway there, her fancy was caught by something trustworthy about me.

"Hee-heeheehee!" the little girl laughed, her teeth showing and her face raised. She had a school bag on her back and a pair of glasses on her nose that were at least half an inch thick.

"Well, well," I said kindly, "hello there!"

"Hee-he," said the little girl. "Hey, you know the answer, I know you do, how much is nine times seventeen?"

"Nine times seventeen?" I asked, surprised.

"You've got to know it!" the little girl said, bouncing at the knees for emphasis. "All you do all year round is arithmetic!"

"Irene, dear, do you know this gentleman?" Eva was stunned. She had never told the children in school about me or about my work.

"Sure I do," answered the little girl. "He carries a guinea pig in his pocket. Show me your guinea pig, will you, please? Please?"

The whole thing set me back on my heels. I wouldn't like to spend much time near a child like that.

"So now you've finally met my grum little Irene," Eva told me later. On the basis of various traits in her behavior, she ought to be in a special school, Eva told me, but it would be a crime to put her there in view of her intelligence and grades. Special school? If it were up to me, I'd put her in an Extra-Special School, a kid like that.

I've been trying to train the guinea pig, but so far I don't see any progress. How do you call a guinea pig so it would come to you? Back on my father's farm, we used to call rabbits "kut-kut-kut-kut." But guinea pigs are from foreign lands, and there is no call for them in barnyard Czech. So it shouldn't make any difference whether I call it "sooey-sooey" or "chick-chick-chick" or "here, goosey, goosey." First, there should be some mental connection between food and the call. But that's impossible, because at our house, anybody who has a piece of food in his hand and thinks of it, feeds the guinea pig. Pavel goes to bed at night with a book and a handful of apples. He reads, he nibbles, and he throws the apple cores in the cage by his bed. He is better off than a reader-nibbler without guinea pigs by his bed.

When Pavel cleans the cage, he puts the guinea pig in his bed, and accepts a swat for it. If he sometimes wants to avoid getting swatted, he comes over to one or another of us and asks, "Does anybody want this beautiful little Albínek for a while?"

I sometimes take the little creature and put it in the pocket of the jacket I wear around the house. If you're going to stick a guinea pig in your pocket, or any place else for that matter, you have to put it in head first, and let it turn around in there by itself. You couldn't possibly get a guinea pig in any hole butt first. It will spread its legs in a petrified spasm, and it's like trying to stuff a hedgehog into a sweater backwards. Head first? Sure, no problem. Then it sits in my pocket without a word, and I walk around, thinking about problems. I try to keep my hand in the pocket with it, so it would feel warm and secure.

Sometimes I take it and put it on the table where Eva and I are drinking our tea. Eva observes the guinea pig, and thinks, what about, I don't know. As for me, I think about the guinea pigs, and I try to coax it back onto my hand. The guinea pig squats in place for a while, and then it starts to sort of cluck, looking around jerkily with a rather glassy eye. Then it screws up its courage to move the position of one foot or another, so it could pick itself up a little, until finally it sets out creeping to investigate the island on which it was cast by some unknown force. It feels the heat of a cup of tea from a distance, it leans its hind legs on the ground, raises its head and with a wriggle of its nose snuffles a trace of steam in the air. Away! Quick! It circumnavigates the sugar bowl without stopping to wonder what is in it. If a spoon happens to clink against a saucer, the guinea pig jerks as if it had been slapped. Further clinks, intentional this time, make it twitch its pink ear. Eva can't watch, she is convinced that the sharp noise hurts its ears, she asks me to cut it out. So I cut it out.

A stroll around the tea table shows the guinea pig to be an interesting spectacle, whereupon I sometimes pick up the creature and carry it on the palm of my hand back to its cage. I am hoping that he will begin to recognize that palm as a promise of a happy return home, and that someday he will decide to climb on it of his own accord. Once at home, the guinea pig immediately departs for a corner of his cage, and there, almost unnoticeably, relieves himself in a manner that borders on the refined. I see in this the expression of some sort of nobility of his species. Can you imagine setting a hen on a tablecloth among the teacups?

My colleague Mr. Karásek asked me how our guinea pig was doing. I said that we liked it fine, but it was hardly doing anything, and I was surprised that it didn't do anything. He remarked that guinea pigs aren't very bright. I asked him how it is that his guinea pig climbs on his hand voluntarily, while mine won't. He didn't answer, and I thought that he hadn't heard my question. At quitting time, when we were locking our desks, I told him that I always used to look forward to quitting time in the evenings, but that now I looked forward even more to getting home. Mr. Karásek nodded that he understood, that he knew. I asked him again how it is that his guinea pig climbs on his hand while mine won't. He was just changing his shoes under his desk, and then went to put on his jacket over by the wardrobe. It wasn't until he was through with all this that he replied, "Put it on a hot kitchen stove, friend, and then put out your hand."

Then he said good night and hurried home.

The inevitable finally happened. Pavel asked whether it was a male or a female that we had. It's a male, but I answered Pavel that it didn't make any difference.

"It does too," he objected, "because if it was a female, we could let it get impregnated."

"Impregnated? But we aren't planning on keeping a rabbit farm."

"No rabbit farm, Dad, but we could fit at least one baby in there," he said. "And if she had a bigger litter, we could sell them to the people you bought Albínek from."

"The Christ Child brought Albínek," Vašek informed his younger brother.

"I don't believe in making a business out of living creatures," I said.

"Well, then, I'd give them away in school," said Pavel.

"Besides, it's all just clinical debate, because Albínek is a male."

"I'll tell you, Dad, I don't think you looked very carefully, or something. Let me show you."

Pavel turned Albínek belly up. The creature kicked its front paws in the air and its hind ones against the table, twisted its head back and forth and chattered its tiny incisors.

"See those little nipples?"

"For heavens sake, we've all three of us got nipples like that!" I exclaimed. Eva wasn't home.

"And so where can you tell?" asked Pavel.

I took the animal, spread the fur on its little behind, turning it toward Vašek, because he is older. But Vašek said, "You can't tell anything there. We looked already."

And he was right; in view of the limited space and the small

30

dimensions, a layman is hard put to determine anything. I was doubtful myself. I would have to see a female, for the sake of comparison. "It's a male," I said.

"And if it were a female, Dad, would it be all right if we kept at least one baby, if it had babies?" asked Pavel.

"You can keep all the babies that this male drops," I said, and dropped Albínek into his cage. The expression on Pavel's face was like what I imagine on the face of the Virgin Mary after the Annunciation.

"In that case, I'd like to have a cat," said Vašek alias Herod, and retreated under the table to his construction site.

Late that night, when the boys were asleep and Eva was grading papers in her room, I started on my accounting again and I thought of my colleague Karásek. How hot does that stove have to be? When Eva said good night and turned off her light, I went for the guinea pig. I dug it out of its half-eaten single. It must have been sleeping like a log; it didn't even squirm. I carried it to the light and placed it on the desk. It squatted there stiff and sleepy, waiting a few minutes before it rearranged its limbs by pulling all the legs that had been scattered around it under itself. It guggled a little in its throat and set out to sniff the papers and books. It walked around with many pusillanimous grumbles. I glanced around the room, until my eyes fell on the coffee table with its transparent glass surface. I picked up the guinea pig from the desk and placed it on the table. Never in its life had it stood on a glass surface. It opened its red eyes in astonishment and began to tremble weakly. The claws on one of its misplaced hind legs quivered a mild tattoo against the glass. I looked at my wrist watch. I waited. It was not until fifteen minutes later that the guinea pig dared to raise its little behind to hide the ill-placed leg. Now it was sitting in its most hostile and alienated stance. In this position, a guinea pig is its shortest ever. First comes its head, and very shortly thereafter comes the definitive end of the guinea pig. It looks like a rabbit that didn't turn out right. Its proportions are wrong, it isn't pleasant to look at. In motion a guinea pig is twice as long, but then it looks rather like a squirrel that didn't turn out right. It has the hind legs of a mole, and it lacks any sort of aesthetic final flourish. The guinea pig sat there as if it were made out of plaster. The cold of the glass made it ruffle its fur up a little, once, and then again, silently, except for what seemed like a profound hiccup, and then it just sat there and sat there. I placed the palm of my hand next to the edge of the glass top of the coffee table. The guinea pig didn't see it. I placed it directly in front of the creature. It was as if it were molded of plaster. I pushed my hand over to touch the toes on its front leg. It didn't budge, it didn't blink, it only retracted its paw by about two millimeters so it wouldn't be touching me. I looked at my wrist watch. I waited fifteen minutes. Then I inclined my head and touched the glass plate with my forehead. It was cool.

Something tickled my hair. Something gave a weak cluck. It was walking around my head, messing with my fur and trying to climb into the warmth. I raised my face, and my eyes were directly in front of the raised and half-opened mouth of a very tiny animal. Its rabbity cleft displayed two shiny mouse-like teeth, its long white whiskers were quivering, and the pink fuzzy nostrils looked as if they were in a draft.

I picked up Pavel's Albínek in both my hands, breathed on him warmly, kissed the top of his head to see if I could do it, and released him at that late hour into his home. Before I left, I asked him please not to tell anybody about it the next day.

When I came home from work a few days later, Eva announced angrily that we had another guinea pig, that I shouldn't have allowed it, and that the animal had to go. I said that I hadn't allowed anything, and asked why it had to go. Eva said that it was a terribly wild creature that wasn't the least bit like Albínek. It wasn't an animal for a city apartment, and that everybody had been chasing him out from behind closets, under beds, behind the bathtub, inside the laundry basket and in the drain. I just stopped long enough to take off my hat and shoes and ran into the menagerie in my overcoat.

"Pavel! What do you think you're doing"

He was sitting disconsolately over his arithmetic book and, with a helpless air, was doing his homework or something.

32

"We've got a new guinea piglet," he said wanly and rose politely from his chair.

"Why have we got a new guinea piglet? That's what I want to hear more than anything."

"You said that I could keep one of Albínek's babies. And for that. . . for that we need a male piglet."

"We have one! Albínek is a male!" I said.

Whenever Pavel and I have one of these sharp exchanges, Vašek always walks around us silently, waiting, pleasantly stimulated by a matter that doesn't concern him, until I take Pavel and wallop him. That's because Vašek himself can only wallop him so that no one notices, and Pavel won't yell very loud, because when Pavel lets out a yell and I come roaring in, there is no telling who is going to get punished after my brief and less than thorough investigation. Sometimes I get angry at what Pavel did, but sometimes I am even more enraged by the fact that Vašek took it upon himself to punish him. Generally, though, I am the angriest for having to become involved in their dispute at all. For Vašek, it is best when Pavel gets into a conflict with me directly. Then he just walks around, smiling and waiting. But I'm not willing to beat one of them just to please the other any more, and mainly I don't want to dish out wallops when I don't know whose idea it was. Sometimes I even try to make Vašek the loser in my controversy with Pavel.

So I shouted, "Albínek is a male!"

"That's what I told him," said Vašek.

"What's that? The other day you still said that you couldn't tell."

"That's right. And that you said that it was a male anyway, that's what I told him."

"You know what? You keep quiet, starting right now, do you hear?"

Vašek began to walk around the room in silence again, slapping a ruler against his palm.

Pavel said, "But Dad, I was counting on Albínek being a male. But at the same time, I asked myself what if he is a female? So I arranged it to work out either way."

"So what did you get? A male or a female?"

I leaned over the cage, but all I could see there was a single animal, white, with red eyes.

"I simply got a guinea pig that was as far different from Albínek as I could find. Look for yourself, it has a slightly different shape, and its behavior is altogether different. Take a look!" And he nodded shyly towards the cage.

I looked again, and there, in the shadow, sitting and eating in the corner, sure enough, there it was. Its color was like camouflage—reddish, with black spots. I reached for it. The new guinea pig began dashing around wildly, jumping over my hand; it kicked the grain dish aside, flew into Albínek's box and shot out of it on the other side. It even tried to climb straight up the wall of the cage. In the meantime, Albínek sat terrified in the corner, letting himself get trampled upon. Finally I grabbed the new one and took it up to the light. It was a bit smaller than Albínek, its head was black, its body red and its legs black. It had bright, clever, black eyes. Where Albínek's eyes always reminded me of the lens of a camera—seeing a sum total of everything and nothing in particular—this creature had a glance that was focussed, centered, black. And where our Albínek's bare skin was pink, this creature's was black. It thrashed about wildly, scratching with its claws, twisting its head like a wild thing, trying to reach my hand with its teeth. I was holding it under its front paws, but it twisted out of my grasp and ended up hanging by its head from my hand. I threw it back into the cage in a hurry. I saw that it was a beautiful animal. It looked as if it had been freshly imported from Peru.

"Well, I don't know," I said, "I'm going to have to talk it over with your mother."

"Talk it over so it turns out all right," Pavel suggested.

That day we all left the new guinea pig alone so it could calm down. We just went in to take a look at it once in a while. We wondered what it was, all four of us.

Later that night, when the boys were asleep and Eva had turned off her light too, I was still sitting over my calculations as usual. I thought of my colleague Karásek, and went into the children's room to take a look at the guinea piglets. The dozing Albínek was braving the elements in the corner of the cage, because his private roomlet was sublet to some wild beastlet. I picked up the little room and righteously dumped the interloper out onto my palmlet. I carried it next door and put it on the tablecloth under the light. The animal crouched as if to make a leap, its little snout twitching; it was even moving its bald black ears. Because I was standing right behind it, it kept turning its head to look at me over its shoulder, first the right shoulder, then the left one. It waited a few seconds before it began to creep over my papers to the edge of the desk. It walked around the island where it had been cast by some unknown force . . . and it was simply preparing to cast off from it. It leaned over the edge of the table, spread its hind legs, alternating its weight from one to the other, making up its mind. A creature that tiny could hurt itself falling from such a height, and so I ran around the table in order to keep it from leaping into the abyss. Like a bolt of lightning or a mouse—that invisibily—because you're not even sure if it was ever there at all—it flew back across the whole desk, sweeping away my partially completed state budget, jumped onto the chair and onto the floor. I kept staring for a while afterward. Some vestige of perception on my retina told me that it had probably fled behind the radiator.

Right. I succeeded in chasing it under a pipe and catching it. I picked it up, stroked it and spoke softly to it, saying that it shouldn't be afraid, little silly thing. I looked it over to make sure that it was all right. It was only frightened, breathing like a pinwheel, and under its delicate ribs, its tiny heart was pulsing like a lady's fine wrist watch. I could have returned it to the cage, but I decided it would be better to take it over to the coffee table and place it on the glass. It froze. It had never stood on anything like it in its life. I thought I could see its fur ruffle up a little. It blinked its eyes, each one separately. It twitched the whiskers on its nose. All of a sudden, its claws scratched the glass, and even though acceleration was a bit of a problem at first, it disappeared before I could even reach out for it. It jumped to one side and landed on the floor where it lay stunned for a couple of seconds. Then slowly, or comparatively slowly, it crept into the corner. It wasn't difficult to catch it there. It didn't even try to prevent me. I examined it and carried it off to the cage. It squeezed into the box next to Albínek. That's the way they stayed, and that is all I know.

I noticed that I was very excited. I wished that it had never happened. If only I had gone to sleep instead.

V

In the days that followed, things didn't look too well for the new little guinea pig. I don't feel like talking about pets, let's talk about the bank.

Things look pretty bad in the bank, but there it isn't my fault. The guards confiscate money from everybody and put it someplace where it is never heard of again. Mr. Chlebeček, the specialist who is our last expert on the subject of lombard, has sown a rumor among us! He says that we are on the verge of a depression. It will start out with an increasing number of bank-notes disappearing from circulation, thanks to the efforts of the bank guards, so that at first a certain amount of merchandise will not get bought, and will remain on the shelves in stores and then in warehouses, and will finally pile up in factory yards. There will be layoffs, not only in our State Bank but everywhere, and the people who get laid off will no longer be able to afford to buy the goods that will be piling up, and so the goods will pile up all the more. In short, a classical depression, the kind you do not read about any more except in school. A depression is a whirlpool, starting with an innocent ripple on the smooth surface

37

of water; it gets deeper and broader, it keeps revolving more and more rapidly, it engulfs air and objects that happen to be in the water, it hisses, it rumbles and finally it roars. I read a good description of an economic depression like that once, in some specialized literature. I am sorely tempted to quote it here:

"As the old man spoke, I became aware of a loud and gradually increasing sound, like the moaning of a vast herd of buffaloes upon an American prairie; and at the same moment I perceived that what seamen term the chopping character of the ocean beneath us, was rapidly changing into a current which set to the eastward. Even while I gazed, this current acquired a monstrous velocity. Each moment added to its speed—to its headlong impetuosity . . .

"The edge of the whirl was represented by a broad belt of gleaming spray; but no particle of this slipped into the mouth of the terrific funnel, whose interior, as far as the eye could fathom it, was a smooth, shining, and jet black wall of water, inclined to the horizon at an angle of some forty-five degrees, speeding dizzily round and round with a swaying and sweltering motion, and sending forth to the winds an appalling voice, half shriek, half roar, such as not even the mighty cataract of Niagara ever lifts up in its agony to Heaven.

"The mountain trembled to its very base, and the rock rocked. I threw myself upon my face and clung to the scant herbage in an excess of nervous agitation.

'This,' said I at length, to the old man, 'this can be nothing else but the great whirlpool of the Maelstrom.'

'So it is sometimes termed,' said he. 'We Norwegians call it the Moskoe-ström, from the island of Moskoe in the midway.' "

At the outset I had no intention of revealing—and I would never have brought it up—that until recently, they used to call Mr. Chlebeček, the specialist that I mentioned, by the name of Mr. Slobechek. When I first heard this nickname, I was upset. But I finally understood how he came by the name when I began to notice him. He would stand in line for lunch in the bank cafeteria with an ancient, ratty and cracked leather brief-case. Its locks were gone and he had to close it with two straps down the front. Actually, he could only use one of the two straps, because the second strap was on the side of his brief case where he kept his canteen. When it came to his turn in the line, he would take the plate of soup that was prepared on the counter and then he would pass the wide-mouthed canteen across the counter, where they would dump a few more ladlefuls of soup in it. Then he would shove his plate further down along the counter, holding the blue enamelled canteen up by its handle, somewhere near shoulder level, like a miner with his lantern, squeezing his briefcase under his arm with his elbow. With his other hand, he would take the tray with the main course. Then everyone would stop and watch Mr. Slobechek add a dish of fruit or salad to his tray, take a piece of cake on a paper napkin, and try to carry in addition, the canteen. It usually couldn't be managed, so he would leave the canteen standing on the counter, and walk uneasily to the table, with the plate of soup in one hand, the tray in the other. All the way he would keep turning back to his canteen of soup, as if someone were about to steal it. He would look for a table where no one else was sitting, and if he didn't find one, he would sit down just anywhere because he would soon have the table all to himself anyway. Maybe he never even figured out why.

He would place the food on the table and return for the canteen, still carrying his briefcase squeezed under his elbow, unwilling to risk its loss; it looked as if it might have been in his possession since his high school days. He would sit down at the table and place the canteen on the floor, to the right of his chair. He would put the briefcase on his lap and open the strap. Then he would remove a slice of bread from his briefcase and crumble it in his soup. Sometimes, when there were dumplings to go with the main course, he would even crumble a piece of dumpling in his soup, having asked for an extra piece of dump- ling for the purpose at the counter. Once he had finished his soup, he would prepare his main course by cutting everything up with his spoon, and only when it was all mixed together with the gravy would he eat it. Whenever he had his fill and there was still a piece of dumpling left, he would pick the canteen off the floor, place it on the table in front of him and dump the leftovers in the soup. Then he would carefully replace the lid on the canteen, stand it back on the floor, and eat his salad and dessert. He would always clean up his plate meticulously with his spoon, and drink the liquid out of his salad dish. After wiping his mouth with his handkerchief and wrapping his spoon in the towel that originally wrapped the bread, Mr. Chlebeček would put the soup canteen carefully back in his briefcase and leave. He never exchanged a word with anyone.

True, he slurped his soup and smacked his lips, true he even threw dumplings with dill sauce in his beef soup, true, his pants were baggy and his feet smelled, but otherwise he was clean, and so were the collar and cuffs of his white shirt. He was just frayed, very much so, like something dating back to the days of the lombard system. That was why I considered the nickname Slobechek to be an exaggeration. And I would never have brought it up at all, if it weren't for the fact that the nickname suddenly disappeared as if it had been withdrawn from circulation; no one ever used it any more, and instead of Mr. Slobechek they called the venerable financial expert Mr. Maelstrom. Maelstrom sounds so massive and dignified as compared to Slobechek that the latter name seems to me to have been completely erased, completely refuted and invalidated. I took it upon myself to explain its origin, so that I might state the fact of its demise—because it is the demise of Slobechek and the origin of Maelstrom that is the firmest confirmation of the immense response that Mr. Chlebeček's hypotheosis aroused in our bank.

At first, the old gentleman dropped his hypotheosis here and there in passing, in the corridors, riding up or down in the paternoster elevator. But mostly his hypotheosis was heard at the bank's newsstand and tobacconists, located just beyond the revolving doors. A great many people spend a great many hours standing around and smoking up a great deal of money there. It must have been there that the gentleman in question also attracted the attention of the bank's director, who had to pass that way and was always urging the smokers to go to work. I think that their encounter must have been something like this: The director came to his bank one morning, and right behind the door he saw a cluster of bankers who like to come to work early, standing around the newsstand as usual. They were standing in a circle, facing in. He said good morning, they turned their heads, returned his greeting, and he said,

"To work, gentlemen, to work!"

"As soon as we finish," they replied, indicating by raising their cigarettes that they meant as soon as they finished smoking. Whereupon they spun right back into the circle. He stopped and approached them.

"What have you got in there?"

"Mr. Chlebeček here has something interesting."

They stood to one side and let the director join them. In the middle of the circle stood Mr. Chlebeček, his grey overcoat unbuttoned, a black hat on his head, in all probability clutching a sheaf of graph paper in one hand, and in all certainty a cigarette in the other. The briefcase was standing at his feet like a faithful old dog. Out of embarrassment, the director shook his hand, saying, "Well, well, what have we here?"

Upon this the engineer repeated for him what he had just told his colleagues, and the director invited him into his office. He offered him a seat in an armchair and said, "Please, tell me once more. I didn't quite understand it all downstairs, and I didn't feel like asking any questions with that bunch of crooks down there."

Several days later, the director had us all assemble, and, as usual, brought up the subject of our stealing.

"Will you finally stop your stealing!" he cried.

A few voices from the back of the room asked, "Why us?"

The director replied, "Do you want to hear? All right Chlebeček, tell them."

The old gentleman was prepared. He had written down the speech in which he was now able, for the first time, to present his hypotheosis in public and in its entirety. I am pleased to present his hypotheosis, or conjecture, for you here in all brevity.

Three levels of monetary circulation have developed in our economy: *controlled* circulation, *recorded* circulation and *myster-*

ious circulation. Controlled circulation is the path by which currency paid out in the controlled pay envelopes of the nation returns to the bank after having been spent. Recorded circulation consists of the process by which currency that we steal, ends up once more at the bank—through shops, movie theaters and trolley cars. Mysterious circulation involves currency that we steal but that is confiscated and vanishes without a trace.

Maelstrom stopped at the third category. He inserted an explanation of the origin and progress of a depression, as I have described it earlier in this chapter, and then he gave voice to his fear: In the resulting depression, someone unknown could come along and throw all the vanished money back into circulation someplace that would pull the entire economy any way that he wants. An extreme example would be if the money got abroad. What could we expect then? And when? The old gentleman got to this point, paused, and said, "And now, my honored colleagues, I will tell you what, in my opinion, must be done, without delay."

"Stop! Shut up! That's enough!" exclaimed the director at that point.

The hand in which the old gentleman was holding his notes dropped to his side. Undecidedly, he turned to the director, then back to us, and by then someone had already walked up to him, gently removed the papers from his hand, and presented them to the director. The old man flushed, gestured stiffly with his right hand, and then turned back to the audience in the hall, crying, "I'm warning you! It's a whirlpool! It's a—Maelstrom!"

He turned, climbed down from the platform, and as he walked past the director, he raised a fragile fist at him, shouting, "I'll write it up again, I will. I can, you know!"

And he left the hall. The assembly was over.

When Mr. Chlebeček concluded his cool exposé with the angry exclamation, "It's a Maelstrom!" I don't think there were very many among the bankers who understood him entirely—for example, my colleague Karásek. As for me, I froze. A vague feeling of anxiety dating back to my youth was grappling its way into my consciousness and I couldn't quite figure out what it meant.

Not until late that night at home—when I was doing my home-work, and when I took a break to observe the guinea pig on the tablecloth—not until then did I realize where I knew that terrible word from. The first clue was an expression that came to my mind: "a descent into the Maelstrom". But why? What kind of a descent? Who? My eyes wandered to the bookshelf, and at that moment I remembered: "A Descent into the Maelstrom" is the title of an outstanding study written by an American economist of the early nineteenth century by the name of E. A. Poe.

I looked it up; I have a copy of the Czech translation, and I read it through carefully. I was once again captivated by the thrilling description of the cold horror experienced by a person encountering the Maelstrom. Poe's study is also the source of the quotation that I presented earlier in this chapter.

I slept badly that night. I couldn't escape the thought that Mr. Chlebeček might be right and that we were all beginning to revolve on the outer rim of a whirlpool like that. At one point between sleeping and waking I thought that an excellent solution would be if I filed my resignation with the State Bank. But when I remembered it in the morning, I realized that it was a lot of nonsense. Where else would I find a job with so much money going through my hands?

Besides, nothing turns out as bad as it seems at the start: every dish of porridge ultimately cools off, according to an old Czech saying. Most clouds don't bring rain, most rifles don't have any effect on the streamrolling of highways. Another thing that had its effect on me was the fact that everyone was maintaining his old equilibrium, as if no depression were imminent. True, the entire State band, yes, everyone, was talking about Mr. Mael-strom's hypotheosis, but everyone kept right on stealing money and the guards kept right on confiscating it. There was a great deal of activity in front of the newsstand and tobacconists. Only, old Mr. Maelstrom didn't stop to talk with anyone any more; he would disappear silently into his office someplace upstairs as if he were insulted by everything that had happened, and no one saw him anywhere except at lunch. What was he doing?

Another thing that contributed to my false calm, was the fact that my fear disappeared without cause. It was my daily guinea pig watching. A guinea pig sits, nibbles at its hay, wiggles its nose, and that is the way it has acted for ages. It is a seductive thought: it makes a man want to believe in the stability of other things, things not in the least bit resembling the activity of a guinea pig. It made me think that perhaps E. A. Poe had simply invented the Maelstrom, and that either nothing of the sort had ever existed in the world, or else it had, but only briefly, in the nineteenth century. Tell me, does the Maelstrom exist to this day? If not, then perhaps we have nothing to fear. I said to myself that I ought to look at some maps, but I kept putting it off from day to day.

One day I went to lunch. I stood in line and moved mechanically closer and closer to my lunch. I happened to turn around, and I was startled to find Mr. Maelstrom standing behind me. His cheeks were flushed with age, and they formed wrinkled pouches that hung from his cheekbones as from a pair of auxiliary struts. His bloodless, bluish lips kept moving in an unconscious whisper. But it wasn't a whisper, it was the effort that the man had to exert to keep renewing the shape of his mouth, because without such effort his lips, on their own, would probably have fallen apart and hung there, half open and corpselike. I also had a moment to notice, at close quarters, the expression of his eyes: they were shiny with tears, and murky; the whites were yellow, the irises gray, and in the middle there were tiny, pointy dots, the pupils. They frightened me as something evil and I looked away; I turned back in the direction of the motion of the lunch line but those eyes stayed clear in my mind for a while, and as I analyzed them, I came to the conclusion that they were not evil. I realized that what had at first appeared to be evil was the result of a certain lack of circumspection, which caused the eyes simply to gaze, their only function the bare one of looking; they were the last, ever-diminishing opening into a soul locked hopelessly inside hollow bone—locked up without any chance of communicating with anyone any more, without hope of any such communication; because to whom could he go? What language could he use, what language of which decade of which regime? For what purpose?

Did he even need to talk any more? Or was it the people around him who needed to hear him? As I glanced around the cafeteria, with its happy chatter, its clinking of dishes, the giggling of the young typists at the buffet counter, I found I could say with one hundred per cent certainty that everyone here at the bank was convinced that he didn't need to hear anything an old coot like him had to say. I didn't turn round any more, but kept advancing in line, and I could hear him push his canteen along the counter—the blue wide-mouthed canteen—and I could feel the corner of his briefcase occasionally touch my back—a worn briefcase, a boy's briefcase from high school.

That very same day I set out to the Map Section of the University Library, where I had them show me all the maps. No, the Maelstrom was not to be found anywhere on the maps. But Poe did write that the people there call it the Moskoestrom, after an island called Moskoe. No, there was no island by that name to be found either. Not even an island with the mouthful of a name of Vurrgh, that Poe mentions as well: "Farther off—between Moskoe and Vurrgh—are Otterholm, Flimen, Sandflesen, and Skarholm. Do you hear any thing? Do you see any change in the water?" But I couldn't hear a thing on any of the maps they showed me, nor could I see anything. I wanted to forgo any further map searching when they handed me, in a rather supercilious manner, a very ordinary, cheap map—a highway map for motorists, but it was very detailed, because it showed all the gasoline stations. This map was not published in the nineteenth century, no, it was dated last year, in short, a very valid map. I found the section that contained the Lofoten, and my eye was struck by the name of an island: Moskenesøy. Isn't that the same as Moskoe? And to the south of it, an island Vaerøy. Isn't Vaerøy the same as Vurrgh? Alas, it is, because in the given space there are four nameless tiny islands just as Poe described them. And above them . . . above them the malevolent word had been hissing at me the whole time: Moskenstraumen! And that is nothing else but the Moskoestrom, or Poe's Maelstrom. It exists! Last year. This year. No figment of the romantic imagination of a romantic century and the early stages of capitalism.

Having made a discovery like that, what should one actually do? After this discovery of mine, my friends, let's all look around for a barrel.

I decided that at lunch the next day, I would approach Mr. Chlebeček. Perhaps I would sit down at the table with him, which is something that no one has ever done, and ask him what he is so silent about. But would you believe it, the next day Mr. Chlebeček didn't turn up at lunch. Coincidence?

I was incapable of any activity, even something as mechanical as turning hundred-crown bills so that the pictures would all be facing the same way. I had to get up from my desk and go away. I rode up to the seventh floor. All the way to where Mr. Maelstrom's office was, under the eaves. The hallways here are narrower than in the lower storeys, because the whole bank gets narrower as it gets taller. A row of doors to the left and to the right. Old brass doorknobs. The floorboards creak. If I were to change my mind and not enter one of the doors, now that I had set all the corridor creaking, many a quiet eyebrow would be raised in the offices behind the doors, in mute surprise.

I knocked on the door numbered 706. No one answered. But let us not presume good hearing in an old gentleman. I knocked again, again nothing; I turned the knob but the door was locked. The key was in the door from the outside. I glanced around, turned the key and entered.

I found myself in a short room with a lower ceiling than we had downstairs, and with a smaller window, too. There were only three pieces of furniture in the room. The desk stood closest to the window. It was an interesting desk, an old-fashioned one. The working area was superposed by rows and rows of pigeon-holes and compartments for papers, with a little railing topping off the archaic structure. A desk of the type I used to see at post offices and railroad stations when I was a child in the country. I remember noticing, too, that a bunch of keys was hanging from one of the drawers. There was a chair in the office, a rounded chair with a caned back. It was pushed back from the desk. And the third item of furniture in the room was a wardrobe, black and towering.

46

The left half of the door to the wardrobe was open, so I could see the familiar gray coat and black hat that the old gentleman wore, but what's more, there was the blue canteen. I dared to approach the wardrobe. I weighed the canteen in my hand. It was empty. He had really not gone to lunch today. But of course, all the time I was listening uneasily to the sounds in the corridor. Slam! In my excitement and in the effort to conceal all traces of my presence here and to leave quickly, I shut the wardrobe, forgetting that I wasn't the one who had opened it. And when I shut the wardrobe, when I closed the left wing of the door that had been open to the side of the desk, I uncovered the space between the desk and the wall. A space that I would otherwise have never thought of examining. What I found in the corner behind the old gentleman's desk filled me with astonishment.

VI

The following day the red guinea pig was conspicuously re-strained. It didn't even try to scale the walls of the cage whenever we placed a hand in the cage. Pavel was pleased.

"He is getting used to us."

Vašek declared cheerfully: "Our two little males have finally made friends."

"They can't both be males," said Pavel.

"They must be," said Vašek.

"They needn't!" Pavel barked, but softly, so he wouldn't get bawled out.

"The both of them have to be males," maintained Vašek fearlessly in my presence.

"Stop arguing, or else," I said, "the both of you males are going to get it."

I reached into the cage. The red one ran over to the white one, pressed up against it and waited. I stroked its head. It bent its head to the floor and let me. I stroked the other, calm and educated animal, scratched it between the ears; it even moved its head to make it easier for me. Was it turning self-indulgent?

48

Then I picked the rusty guinea pig up. It squirmed, it scratched me a little, it twitched its legs in the air until it found them resting on the palm of my other hand. Then it pulled itself together into the smallest possible volume and looked around, its head jerking like a chicken's. In a similar situation, Albínek clucks and squeals, whereas this specimen of the Peruvian Guinea Pig (*Cavia porcellanus*) is silent. We have yet to hear its voice. I stuck the new guinea pig in my pocket and went to my room with it, where I proceeded to pace and meditate on problems. In order that the guinea pig should feel warm and secure, I kept my hand on it in my pocket.

I thought about the bank and things: about my colleague Mr. Karásek, about Mr. Maelstrom's hypotheosis, about trousers at half-mast and revolving doors, the state budget and about money. But I also recall a thought about a fiddle passing through my mind. The guinea pig in my pocket was a pleasant feeling, while the thought that I would have to go back to my figures was an unpleasant one. I thought of Eva's crazy pupil and I felt uncomfortable. Not that it really matters what nine times seventeen is. It's a hundred and fifty three. What brought on a certain degree of anxiety was the fact that she could see into my pocket, because it so happens that I did have a guinea pig in my pocket, which even Eva wasn't aware of. That little girl really haunted me. The guinea pig in my pocket pleased me. I recalled a question I was asked by my colleague Mr. Karásek: "Well, friend, have you discovered the significance of guinea pigs yet?"

I took the creature out of my pocket and walked over to the window with it. I raised it up on the palm of my hand, and looked up at it, contemplating its shape, size, color. and fear. It was very lovely and I could see that it was in fact significant, it had everything: eyes, a short life in this world; and if I were to let it drop to the floor from that altitude, all I could have done would have been to leave home and roam the black streets of the city.

In the meantime, the argument was continuing, mutedly, beyond the door. "He must be a male, too," Vašek stated pointedly in a manner inherited from the teachers' estate.

"Why do you have to keep saying that over and over like an

idiot, you idiot!" Pavel barked irritably and I could see, even though there was a wall and a door between us, how he was trying to kick Vašek in the shins under the table. They were sitting opposite each other doing their homework. "Why do you keep repeating it like an idiot?" he wailed helplessly.

"Because the only thing that he can be is just a male, that's all. Because you said, 'He might be a female,' and all I said was 'He can't.' You ought to have said, 'She might be a female.' That's all. You started out by saying 'he . . . .'" Vašek was explaining his logic, only to be interrupted by a wail.

"Stoooopid!" and Pavel was crying.

I hid the guinea pig in my pocket and burst into the menagerie in the best of moods to light into the two of them. But my hand was restrained by a doubt, and so I did something even better.

"You can do better than that," I said to Pavel, and from his notebook, I ripped a page with what I saw to be a sloppily written homework assignment. I turned to Vašek and said, "Only a fool calls attention to how smart he is in times of stress!" and I ripped a page out of his notebook too.

I went to the kitchen. Eva was fixing dinner—pancakes. I sat down at the table and set the little guinea piglet on the table. The rusty head ducked under the edge of a plate that was set there.

"I still can't find out what it is," I said.

"A male, if you want to go by behavior," said Eva from where she was standing by the stove.

"That doesn't mean anything," I said. "It might just have different parentage or different training."

The guinea pig was crawling carefully along the edge of the table. Occasionally it would raise its nose in the air and sniff. The smells in the air as well as the noises, the frying hisses, disturbed it. "I don't belong here, I don't belong here, my God, how did I ever get here," that's what it was trying to say to itself, but it didn't know how to.

"It's really a lovely, delicate thing," said Eva, "but something makes me want to poke a finger in its eye."

"You won't do it, now that you've said it."

"You know I wouldn't poke it, for heaven's sake."

"But it would be on your mind all the time."

"And what's on your mind all the time around those guinea pigs?" she asked me.

"All sorts of things. Your pancakes are burning. But it was a great idea, giving the boys a guinea pig for Christmas, wasn't it? Now they think more about living things. I just ripped a page out of their notebooks."

"Did you ever see Pavel playing with Albínek? He puts him on the couch and puts his face right up to him. Albínek runs around, his head like a little piggie turned loose from the sty. He jumps up, crumples in the air and falls down all crooked, then he begins to lick Pavel's eyebrows, and then he starts to run around, wiggling his little rear end. Pavel is the only person he plays with like that."

"No, I never saw that. Karásek at the bank told me that his guinea pig shinnies up his arm all the way to his shoulder. He probably trained it. But if you train an animal, you don't know what it's really like. What's that crazy little girl of yours doing?" I asked.

"That child scares me. I'm even afraid to call on her in class because I never know what she's going to say," said Eva.

"There's a commercial engineer at the bank and he's come up with some sort of hypotheosis about a depression," I said, and settled down to tell her about it.

"Hypotheosis? You mean hypothesis, don't you?" said Eva.

"I know it's a hypothesis as well as you do. But I'm not going to say another word."

"What kind of a depression? Another one?" She was inquisitive.

"I'm not going to tell you another word!" I said.

"Do you have to take and rip pages out of their notebooks for no reason at all?" she asked.

"Next time I'll wallop them."

"Or do you have to beat them?" She was upset.

"You might at least teach all those brats in school, each and every one of them, to write," I said.

51

I picked up the guinea pig, crammed it into my pocket and left the room. I lay down on the floor and placed the guinea pig on my stomach. I made a coral around it with my arms. It walked all over me, looking for a corner. It nuzzled in my armpit. It needed peace and quiet, well, so did I, but there was a lot of racket everywhere. I thought about how being picked up by some unknown force and being lifted high up in the air must terrify a guinea pig! In their native habitat, no guinea pig ever survived an experience like that, because it was always an indication of an encounter with a beast of prey. The end. And life goes on, you are here, my dear. But let's not anthropomorphize. And don't get literary either, because mortal terror, I mean fatal terror is something that an animal can't pass on to its heirs as an instinct. A guinea pig, when lifted into the air, feels around with its legs and prepares itself for a fall. It stands many chances of falling during its life, but not of dying. Fear of death prior to death is something that has been reserved for mankind. And if it is the truth that at the moment of his death, a man executed by hanging emits his seed, an alert woman could conceivably give birth to people who would feel uncomfortable at the mere sight of the gallows.

But let's not talk about gallows, children, let's talk about pets, they are closer to the ground. I turned the guinea piglet belly up and held one of its black paws. It was a front paw, consisting of four pointy fingers ending in claws, dull and peeling, a pudgy palm with deep wrinkles and a hard pillow instead of its fifth digit. A guinea pig has only three digits on its hind paws. The creature's fingers were spread into a fan shape, and it probably didn't even know it. It was breathing hard, with a frequency of three breaths per second; it was grinding its little teeth, turning its head back and forth, wheezing weakly with the effort. I touched its palm with a pencil: the fingers pulled together until they formed some sort of a cup. But they couldn't bend in all the way and close; the creature had never picked anything up in its paws, and never climbed along a branch. I removed the pencil and the fingers spread wide again, and the piglet didn't even know about it. Did I tell you that it has ears too? Didn't I? The guinea pig's ears aren't like the big flaps that rabbits and hares have, but they aren't like a cat's tiny pointy ears either. Guinea pigs' ears resemble nothing so much as human ears, monkeys' ears, and your ears. They are approximately kidney shaped, they are thin and delicate and they are very good at hearing. Albínek can tell by the sound of his footsteps that it is Vašek who is coming into the menagerie and so he knows that it is senseless to start to cry for food. He can tell by the footsteps when I am the one coming, and calls out from a distance, "Aw, go look it up in a book someplace and let me be!"

The rusty guinea pig, so wild only a day ago, and so conspicuously tame today, was creeping all over my stomach, trying to find a hiding place. Wouldn't you have loosened your jacket too, and undone a button on your shirt? Wouldn't you? Well, that's what happened at our house. Feeling the gentle warm creature on your bare skin is an absolutely unique experience; it is a luxury verging on the atavistic, something forgotten, primitive, and sweet; you want to wind yourself around the little animal, but it's too small for that; you can't curl up that small, your capacity for cuddling is obviously unutilized. Well, do what you can.

Eva walked in and said, "We can eat dinner now. Call the boys, will you?"

"No, we can't," I said. "Not till we get ourselves up."

"Then get yourselves up."

"We can't. We've got something under our shirt."

She came closer, knelt thoughtfully beside me, stuck her hand under my shirt, felt the little animal and said, "Here?"

"No, not there."

"Oh, here!" she said.

She took the guinea pig out and pitied it. It seemed to have a mournful look about it. I told her that I had been thinking mournful thoughts and that the guinea pig probably felt it.

"Mournful thoughts about what? About me?" she asked.

"All sorts of things, even the gallows," I told her.

"Well, then, now we can eat our supper."

"I want to show you something," I said. "Tell me what it reminds you of." And I showed her the guinea pig's palm.

"A little hand," she replied.

"That's the irreparable fact of it: it will never be a hand, ever."

"I'd be happier if we only had one guinea pig. I wouldn't be so afraid. Why don't you let it go? And call those boys for supper."

She returned to the kitchen. I lay back down on the floor and put the guinea pig on my chest. Then I began to sit up, ever so slowly. The guinea pig kept climbing higher and higher, until it ended up in the hollow of my collarbone. Then I stood up, gradually, and the guinea pig was in the same place as Mr. Karásek's. In this position, I brought it into the children's room.

I sent the boys in to have their supper. As he left the room, Pavel turned to look at me and the guinea pig, but I urged him to kindly move on and do as he's told. I dropped the guinea pig into its cage. I watched it retreat to a corner immediately upon its return home, and then I watched the other guinea pig, the white one, walk over to it, and murmur something to it, face to face. I expect it was asking what they had wanted of it, and whether or not they had done anything to it. I made sure that the rusty guinea pig told the truth, that nothing had happened to it, and then I went in to eat my pancakes too.

At supper, Vašek said, "Dad, won't you get mad at me if I ask you a question? Seriously?"

"I probably will, if you start out like that," I replied.

"Then I had better not ask."

"Why shouldn't you ask?" said Eva indifferently. "If you want to ask, then ask."

"Okay," said Vašek with a smile, "I wanted to ask Dad how can I tell a time of stress."

I thought about it for a while, and then I said, "Would you please bring me that homework assignment that you did over, and the page I tore out?"

"Not now," said Eva. "Let the child at least finish his supper in peace."

"No, that's all right, Mom," said Vašek, "I'll bring it." He brought his notebook and the torn-out page.

"Look at that," I pointed to the notebook, "it's sloppier than it was the first time. I think I'll have you do it over again."

"But you didn't tear it out because it was sloppy, you tore it out because of times of stress."

"Right, and that's why you should have been damned careful to do an even better job than before, since it's a time of stress. And you did a worse job!"

And I tore out the page again.

"I can't stand it" exclaimed Eva.

"But I'm not going to do it over again," Vašek growled.

"Anything you say, pal," I said, "anything you say."

But he did it over again, the good lad, he did do it over again! And I didn't even have to yell at him.

VII

The rusty guinea pig stopped eating.

"Do you think Red is getting sick, Dad?"

"He's probably sick already. That's what you get for messing with him."

"But I didn't mess with him, Dad. At all."

"Did too," I said. "You must have."

The guinea pig cowered in a corner and stared straight ahead. Carrots, parsnip, piece of apple, hay, grain in the dish—it wouldn't touch a thing. I reached out a hand to it. It jerked and scrambled over to another corner with the speed of a healthy guinea pig.

"Don't, Dad!" exclaimed Pavel, grimacing as if he had a bellyache while trying to run the 100 yards dash.

"A cat would have been better," said Vašek glumly.

"No cat, and no more guinea pigs either!" said Eva. "I'm as upset as if I had a sick baby in the house. I keep feeling that we ought to do something."

"Take it to the veterinarian," suggested Vašek.

"You probably don't take animals as small as that to the vet's," said Eva.

Pavel began to weep silently into his milk. He didn't feel at all like going to school. At work, I asked my colleague Karásek what it could mean when a guinea pig doesn't eat for a day.

"It means," he said, "that it's not going to eat any other day either."

"You mean a guinea pig can't just up and simply get sick?" I voiced my objection.

"A guinea pig is a very small animal compared to us," Karásek explained. "Our colds and our piles are so far apart that in between, we can fit sinusitis, a heart attack, a gall bladder, appendicitis . . . But when a guinea pig catches a cold, it gets it along with pneumonia and dysentery all together. And who would treat a guinea pig?"

"Theoretically, it ought to be possible," I said.

"But practically, you'd do best to get yourself a pair and they'll keep manufacturing new ones."

"But we don't want the children to get accustomed to watching death," I said. "Then the guinea pigs would serve the opposite purpose to what we intended in the first place."

He smiled and said, "Friend, you have yet to discover the true purpose of guinea pigs."

I didn't ask.

At noon I entered the canteen directly behind Mr. Maelstrom. I found myself in line behind him. I waited for him to set up camp at one table or another, and then I sat down as close to him as I could to be able to observe him. Well, he ate as was his habit. Essentially, if you consider it without any prejudice whatsoever, you could say that he just has a different set of manners. I didn't even feel a shadow of disgust, just amazement at the volume that he consumed. He is a dry, delicate figure of a man, his chest is shrunken, his shoulders frail, his abdomen a bit protruding. At his age, people hardly eat anything at all, I'm told. Now, he eats a lot, and so what? Maybe he has to eat so terribly much to keep his innards functioning. Or else, he has holes in everything, so that the fuel tumbles out through the holes and emerges essentially untouched, like the oats that feed the meadow larks on roads that are frequented by horses.

But he is a very old man! Strange that he is still around. What does he do all day, and whom does he answer to? How much do they pay him, and will they give him a raise now? Now that they want him to keep his mouth shut, will they give him a raise, or will they pension him off, as soon as possible and with as large a pension as possible? It all depends on his nature. They might also try to liquidate him. That strange discovery that I made in his office, should I tell anyone about it? Or do they know?

I decided to have a talk with the old man. When I finish eating, I could walk over to his table. No, I would do better to wait until he's finished eating, and leave the bank cafeteria with him, and slip into the paternoster with him. I finished my lunch, went and bought myself a soda and read a newspaper article that they had pinned to the bulletin board, before the old gentleman was done. I approached the paternoster just behind him. The cabin that approached had one person in it. The old gentleman stepped in carefully, thus filling the cabin to capacity, and I couldn't ride with him. I watched the dry old figure disappear upward, slowly and passively, up to his waist, his knees, until finally only his black oxfords with their thick rubber soles were all that was visible through the crack; his shoelaces were apparently taken from a pair of military boots. They were long and thick, tied in a double bow with dangling ends. I heaved a sigh of relief. I had tried my best.

When it was quitting time, I walked out of the bank and found Eva waiting for me outside. That doesn't happen often.

"You're here?" I rejoiced. "What's the matter?"

"I'm ashamed of myself," she said, "but I had to come and meet you. The boys are home already."

"Did anything happen?" I asked.

"No, nothing happened, but I'm scared," she said.

"Oh, come on!"

"I forbade them to leave the house, told them not to open any windows and not to touch the kitchen stove, and I decided to come out and get you."

"Then something did happen, damnit?"

"Nothing, I must be silly, but I had to be sure."

"Stop irritating me and tell me what it's all about."

"There isn't any 'it'. That's all. I just wanted to come for you."

I thought of something, and I was insulted. She tried to take my arm, and I pulled away. We walked down Wenceslas Square to the street called Na Můstku, and from there down the avenue called Národní třída. We stopped to look at shop windows. I was getting madder and madder at Eva, I even felt like using a dirty expression that I had picked up someplace, "Speak up or shit letters!"; it was in fact the first time in my life I had a really suitable chance to use it; up till then it had been a useless bit of knowledge. But I didn't use it, because I would have had to blush in front of you, children, when relating this episode to you faithfully. And so I said, as calmly as I could, "Could you please, kindly, tell me something, at least?"

"I had another run-in with that girl at school," she said.

"With the crazy one?"

"That's right. I called on her in class today. I always tell myself I'm not going to bother with her any more, and that I'll just give her a grade, any grade. But then I can't help myself. I think that even though . . ."

"Stick to the subject," I urged her.

"Well, I called on her, she seemed to know the lesson, but what she said was all mixed up, like some seeress or medium or something. I don't know any more if it's just her unconscious manner, or something, because she isn't normal, or whether it's intentional and fresh . . ."

"Stick to the subject . . ."

"Anyway, I told her to answer my question with a whole sentence. I said, 'Irene, in a complete sentence.' And she said, 'What in a complete sentence?' So I said, 'Answer!' And she said, 'Well, then, tell it to me in a complete sentence, okay?' "

"That's fresh, but cute," I said.

"I thought the same thing, and so I said to her, 'Irene, always answer me with a complete sentence, will you please?' "

"What has that got to do with our boys? And the kitchen stove and the window!" I asked.

"Well, wait a minute. I'm sticking to the subject. So when I repeated it in a complete sentence, she just gave me that idiotic look of hers, confused and absent, so I could never tell if she was concentrating on a mental effort or wetting her pants; and then she said, 'You better quit asking me for complete sentences, or else I'll tell you a complete sentence that you'd be better off not hearing.' And so I asked her 'What would I be better off not hearing? What sentence is that?' 'You'd be better off not hearing about his dying.' And then she started to cry and say, 'Yes, yes, somebody's going to up and die on you, teacher, he's going to die!' "

"That's awful, and it's nonsense."

"I think it's stupid too, but all of a sudden I got so scared that I couldn't keep my mind on anything else."

"Nonsense. I'm not crazy, and I can prophesy that there'll be a death in the family too. The guinea pig."

We walked all the way home. She was calm all the rest of the way home, but when we got to our house, she was possessed by such an onslaught of maternal concern that she flew up the stairs, as if to make up for lost time! She rushed into the apartment with a crazed look on her face and frightened the boys.

"What happened?" exclaimed Vašek.

"Nothing. Did something happen?" she asked in return.

"Nothing here either," he replied.

"Pavel, where is Pavel?"

"He's bawling over by the hutch," said Vašek.

Pavel wasn't really bawling, but his face was sort of twisted. It was still alive, but just barely. Its fur was ruffled and its eyes sunken. Its metamorphosis surprised and frightened me: a shiny, agile creature, with bold claws and bright eyes transformed into a sticky blob, trembling feverishly. What frightened me was how real, how immense the shadow of death is, even on such a small body. What's going on? Are you really dying? That means, little creature, that I guessed right, that originally you were really alive. And that you had a right to live. Now all that there is of you as I take you in my hand is a pile of fragile bones under a thin fur coat.

Pavel walked in circles round me, afraid to give voice to the question, which led me to conclude that he still wasn't counting on Red's dying, that he was just afraid, worried, helpless, wondering what to do, convinced that we were wiser. I noticed that Albínek wasn't in the cage. Pavel had moved the other guinea pig into a separate box that he pushed beneath his bed. Albínek was sitting in the hay, nibbling at a carrot, occasionally peeling a strip of paper from the box and eating it with a healthy good appetite.

I wondered whether a guinea pig is in fact too small an animal to be treated. Could anyone help? But should something that is supposed to die be saved? Someone who is supposed to die, if anyone is supposed to die, according to a stupid little girl?

"Isn't there any medicine for animals?" Pavel asked in a tearful voice.

"Maybe there is, but we don't know what kind, and we don't have it."

"If we don't know what kind," he objected, "how can we say that we don't have it. Can we?"

"We have aspirin," said Vašek. "And suppositories."

"That's all a bunch of nonsense!" I said, and sent him to the medicine cabinet for the aspirin.

I crumbled a piece off an aspirin tablet. We opened Red's mouth and, with the help of an eye dropper, placed a few drops of water along with the medicine down the tiny throat. I think that penicillin would have helped; that ought to work on large and small creatures alike. Unless of course there was a bruised kidney. After we had given our poor little patient the aspirin, we turned off the light in the bedroom and left. The boys had already decided to do their homework in the kitchen so that Red could have some peace and quiet, and maybe so they'd be further away from me.

If something is supposed to die, it's going to die, but we ought to try to help it live. When the boys went to bed about two hours later, they came running back with some news that surprised me. The sick guinea pig was walking around and eating. Eva and I hurried in to have a look. The guinea pig retreated to a corner and waited to see what would happen. Eva and I exchanged glances. I knew that she was scared again. I understood, it would naturally be much better if it were a guinea pig that was going to die than if it were something larger. The guinea pig sat for a while, then it turned around with a trembling motion, picked up a blade of hay, and with a grinding motion of his tiny mouth, it began to suck it inside. With its sunken eyes and ruffled fur and the way it was quivering, it looked like somebody who had just gotten a terrible beating, but had remained spiritually unbowed. Its work on the blade of dry grass looked like proud defiance, so much so that it made us want to laugh.

And Pavel was laughing.

VIII

The next morning at breakfast we talked about death. They say that it takes three days to die. I had heard that, so had Eva, only our boys didn't know anything about it. Three days—that goes for a human being. You'd expect the time to be proportionately shorter for a guinea pig. We gave it about a hundredth of an aspirin yesterday. A thoughtful Pavel was drinking his milk; he said sarcastically, "But when they shoot somebody, where are your three days?"

"Three days of what?" asked Eva.

"Of dying."

"That's instantaneous," said Vašek.

"And three days when you get hit by a train?" growled Pavel.

"That's instantaneous too, Mister Smarty Pants."

"And when you drown, Mister Weisenheimer?" he retorted, with milk on his chin and tears in his eyes—sorrowful tears that he was trying to dry up with his fury.

"Quiet and eat!" I replied.

"Who gets three days to die in, nowadays?" said Eva.

"Anybody that has the time," I said.

But it was time to go to work and to school, and so we couldn't continue the debate. The boys always leave at the same time as Eva, even though they go to different schools. I leave the house an hour after they do, because the bank doesn't open until nine o'clock. When they had all left, I played the violin for a while. Still under the influence of our breakfast debate, I played only serious pieces. I walked round and round the table, playing in time to my steps, while in the next room the rusty guinea pig was taking its third day to die.

This morning had been sad in the menagerie. Pavel had gotten dressed with muffled sobbing and Vašek hadn't even tried to tease him; he was also affected by the still unknown impression of someone's dying. After yesterday's surprise improvement in Red's condition, it was a real disappointment for the boys. Pavel wanted to give him the medicine again, but first of all it was hopeless, and secondly Eva asked us for heaven's sake to grant the poor creature one last bit of mercy—the peace to die. Eva remembered, from having been at her grandmother's deathbed as a child, that the dying need to concentrate on their departure, and as long as they are not forcibly brought back to consciousness—which at best means an awareness of their pain or their concern—they no longer suffer. The guinea pig had changed overnight into a ragged clump, its sharp eyes, its speedy feet, had vanished. It was still breathing, occasionally it moved, perhaps in an effort to relieve the pain that it probably barely felt now anyway, semiconscious as it was. There was a moist puddle behind it. An infection, then, rather than an internal injury? Pavel had been wise to separate the creature from Albínek.

Before any of us returns home, the guinea pig will obviously no longer be among the living—Eva and I had prepared the boys for that. But it seemed very strange, very strange indeed, for all of us to leave and to let something stay behind here to perish, to depart for non-existence. I had a feeling that something like that ought to be illegal. Think about it for a moment, my dear young friends, there is nothing more important than dying; and dying alone—when your near and dear ones know about it, but leave you anyway—is dying most unnecessarily, and maybe even

64

unwillingly, but it has to be gone through with, once it is started. How brutal, not to pay attention to one of ours who is dying. And as for someone who dies without having anyone, has he ever lived? Whose was Red? But then, turn that same thought process around and you will see how impossible it sounds: taking the day off from work because our pet guinea pig is dying, because a dumb little beast is croaking.

But it was all useless; I just couldn't get over the feeling that someone should have stayed at home. And yet I would be leaving too, shortly. I stopped playing and took my violin into the children's room. I sat down by the cage. The guinea pig didn't pay any attention to me; it was taken up entirely with its occasional spasms. I plunked the D string. Nothing. No, I won't play for it. A variation in tones could disturb it, even hurt it, if it still was capable of hearing. A melody is an address, a challenge, an aggression. But one constant unchanging t-o-o-o-ne . . . wouldn't that be it? A tone announces nothing, inflicts nothing, and presents no instructions; a tone only has duration and fills up space; it becomes an attribute of the space it fills, its taste, its color, its odor. I have some sort of recollection from my very early childhood: a mountain field, I don't know where, I was there, all around just grass and a t-o-o-o-ne. The sun sho-o-o-ne, the breeze was blo-o-o-wing . . .

I tucked the violin under my chin and began to play, just the way I was, seated on the floor. I played the most beautiful extended chord I know, the G-D fifth. I played it medium-loud, pulled the bow up and down, regularly, up and down and up . . . I don't know how long it took, but everything resounded with that lovely chord, skull, chest, windows, walls. And the guinea pig—I kept looking at the guinea pig—and noticed that it was ceasing to tremble and that it was calming down, until the pain had apparently eased and it had gone to sleep, its tiny chest, rising and falling with regular little breaths.

I left the house feeling satisfied. And because I had just missed my trolley car, I walked to the next stop perfectly willingly and in a mood to make the best of anything that would come my way. I came to the corner of our street, where all the subterranean pipes and cables were being completely changed; there was a pile of yellow clay and a deep excavation full of pipes and cables of various thicknesses, some wrapped with insulation and others unwrapped. The only things missing there were the men at work. You can imagine my surprise when I looked down and saw a boy sitting there, in a blue windbreaker, conspicuous in his resemblance to my older son. I called out to him, "Hi, there! I thought you were in school!"

He looked up, surprised, his resemblance to Vašek becoming even more marked, and said, "Hi. I'm just going."

And he walked down the excavation along the pipes.

"Up here!" I called to him.

"Why? It's shorter this way," he replied.

I ordered him to get the hell out of there immediately, and when he got close enough, I smacked him one behind the ears, because it may have been shorter through the ditch, but it was slower. His feelings were hurt, and that night he denied the whole thing, making Eva testify to the fact that we don't even have a blue windbreaker, and making a fool out of me—which wasn't surprising, because a lot of people at the bank could be thinking the same thing about me.

I want to find out what Mr. Maelstrom had in mind and what the director has on him that is keeping him from talking. The old gentleman walks among us but he doesn't share his hypothesis with anyone any more. People from office to office frighten each other with false conjectures, but no one is even considering a way out. I don't intend to be the director's pet, a collaborator with the powers that be, I won't go around saying, "Don't steal, the director doesn't like it." What would we live on? Not stealing, that's nothing. Not stealing is something that is conceivable, achievable. But not stealing so that there would be some advantage to it would mean drawing many other conclusions with regard to conditions. Yet, no one wants to talk about that now, no one believes in joint action, everybody speaks of bad experiences or uses his wife and family as an excuse, or pretends to be stupid, or is stupid.

"Let's go see Maelstrom together," I suggested to my colleague Mr. Karásek.

"My friend," he replied in a contemptuous tone.

I said, "Aren't you interested in what he wanted to say, friend?"

"Do you really have to hear it?" he replied.

"I think that it would have to be interesting," I said, "even if it's a little old hat."

"The old codger has exhausted his brain already with his babblings," my colleague Karásek said, and he walked out.

It is our job, Karásek's and mine, to arrange the hundred-crown notes. I place them in piles with all the pictures facing the same way, and he arranges them in the order of their serial numbers. This time the bank notes were from the D-62 series. When there is a number missing, he goes around the bank trying to find out whether or not somebody didn't just take it, leaving a leftover bank note from another series in exchange. Because he keeps having to leave for this purpose, our conversations are very spasmodic. We often forget where we left off, and rather begin at the beginning again. Sometimes that's for the best: it's interesting to note how the same conversation can develop entirely differently when one of the participants unwittingly uses a formulation different from the one he did the first time. Our conversation earlier this morning was obviously an insignificant debate about the mental abilities of poor Mr. Maelstrom. But it was interrupted, and when Karásek returned about an hour later with several bank notes of the D-62 series in his hand, we recommenced the conversation.

"Let's go see Maelstrom together," I suggested.

"My friend," he replied in a contemptuous tone, which now showed no small degree of irritation.

I said, "Aren't you at all interested in what he wanted to say, friend?"

"Do you really need to hear it?" he replied, as before.

"It's not so much a matter of whether I need to hear it," I said, "as it is a matter of why the director needed us not to hear it."

"Have you considered why he might have kept him from saying it?" asked Karásek.

"I have. Quite a lot," I said.

"Have you really thought about it in all its aspects, or have you just been revolving around the first idea that occurred to you?" he asked.

I stopped short. I had to admit that I hadn't thought about its different aspects because my first idea had seemed correct and satisfactory. I said, "The director silenced the old man because his proposals and his ideas displeased him."

Karásek looked at me sadly, saying, "Look, friend, I don't feel like talking about it here. Just one thing: There are excellent ideas that become unfeasible by the very fact of their having been proclaimed on the street."

"I understand," I said, but it wasn't the truth, this time I got him wrong. I thought that he was talking about barrels.

"I understand. But one could always order enough barrels fast enough so that there would be enough to go round?"

"I don't understand you, friend."

"Mr. Chlebeček . . . " I said with uncertainty, "I mean, I'm assuming that you have read Poe's *Descent into a Maelstrom* . . . Mr. Chlebeček has a barrel hidden in his office."

He stared at me astonished, not understanding. Then his astonishment turned to amusement.

"Maybe he wants to put up some sauerkraut. And how about your guinea pigs? Are they croaking yet?"

"No. Why? They're just fine. The sick one got better."

I didn't feel like talking with him any more. Soon he left the office again and didn't come back until just before five o'clock. We exchanged cool goodbyes. I stayed behind a little, intentionally, so as not to have to meet him again downstairs. But when I got off the paternoster, I could see him standing by the revolving door as I approached. His hands were clasped over his head, one guard was removing the contents of his pockets, tossing them in a pile at his feet, while a second guard was riffling through the contents of his brief case. Then the first guard permitted him to drop his hands to his sides, and raised his hat. No sooner had he lifted it, than a green bank note slid off Karásek's head and glided like a broad green leaf to my feet. I bent down and handed it to the guard, but I stopped first to glance at the serial number—series D-62. The guard thanked me and waved me on outside, as a reward. As I passed my colleague Mr. Karásek, I remarked, "Well, what do you know, it got found after all. That ought to please you, friend, doesn't it?"

When I arrived home, the guinea pig was still alive. The boys were pleasantly surprised, Eva was standing over it in silent horror. She couldn't concentrate on any of her work, she was waiting excitedly for me to come home, certain that I would make some decision.

"I don't think I can stand it any more," she said. "They say that if someone has committed a grave sin, he finds it difficult to leave the world. But this little creature? I feel guilty that it has to suffer so much, here, with us."

"Maybe it couldn't die because we weren't home," I said.

"But we aren't his family," said Vašek. "I thought maybe we should have left Albínek in with him, but Pavel said no."

"You know you want Albínek to catch it too," Pavel spoke out angrily, "because you want a cat."

"We're not going to have any cats, or guinea pigs either," declared Eva.

"You mean we're going to kill Albínek?" exclaimed Pavel.

"Red is almost certain to have some sort of intestinal infection," I told Vašek. "I don't even know if we'll be able to put Albínek in the cage after him."

"Mom, did you hear what I said? Do you want us to kill Albínek now?" Pavel was enraged.

"Of course, we won't kill him," said Eva. "Why should we kill him, for heaven's sake?"

"Just a little bit," said Vašek.

Pavel pulled his spoon out of his porridge, licked it off, and clink! right on top of Vašek's head. "You're the one we'll kill, and not just a little bit."

"All right, all right," I guided the conversation, "do you want your face slapped?"

Pavel was crying in his porridge and I said, "Let's turn the page and ask our excavation foreman here whether he found his way to school."

Vašek did not react.

"Well?" I asked again.

Pavel wiped his nose and stopped whining, his attention captured by the new matter at hand. Eva gave me a surprised look. Vašek didn't respond in the slightest. When he saw that everyone was looking at him, he looked honestly surprised and said, "What are you talking about? I don't know what you're talking about."

"This morning we exchanged hellos," I said. "Where was that?"

"In the hall," said Vašek.

"And later on, again, in the ditch, eh? First we exchanged hellos and then the back of my hand, right?"

"Gee, it's too bad I wasn't there, if that's the way it was," he said.

Pavel giggled.

"You mean to say that I didn't find you over at the excavation this morning?" I was really asking seriously this time.

"Sorry, Dad, but you really didn't."

I placed my spoon in my porridge in silent astonishment and placed my hands on my hips. I shook my head, clarifying the memory in my mind, fully certain of myself.

"I left for work at half past eight, Mister Wise Guy, I walked past the hole in the street, I looked inside and what do I see? You, sitting on a pipe, a big fat one with insulation wrapped around it. The same eyeglasses, the same mug, and a blue windbreaker."

"These eyeglasses, at half past eight, were sitting on this mug, Dad, in school. And as for a blue windbreaker, I don't own one—at all."

"Since when don't you own a blue windbreaker?"

"Since ever, Dad."

"You must be out of your mind," Eva said to me instead of to Vašek. "We don't have a blue windbreaker, or any blue jacket at home, and we never did have. Who was it you saw wherever you saw him?"

"Him, of course, I boxed his ears!" I defended myself.

But nobody believed anything but the slap, and I got mad and went into the children's room.

The guinea pig didn't even look like an animal any more; it sat there like a fur ball emitted by an owl, half digested. You couldn't see its eyes, it wasn't warm, it was cold. When I touched it with a finger, it didn't budge. When I poked it, it crept on a centimeter or two. I touched it lightly with my finger again. No! But that's really awful. Why? What is it supposed to mean? A blind guinea pig, three days ago still agile, defensive, and so frightened that it could run straight up the walls of its cage, now was creeping like a lame beggar, where to? To me, toward my hand, trembling, tapping its uncovered teeth against the floor like a cripple with a crutch. It was a young thing, it had never seen anything and never would, it would never know anything, it didn't want to die.

Meanwhile, in the box under the bed, the white guinea pig sat and watched calmly, clean and smooth, healthy and stupid. I picked up the white guinea pig, it spread its legs in the air, I sat it in the cage. It looked around uncomfortably, it didn't recognize its home any more because in the last two days it had forgotten its entire education, and then it began to run back and forth from corner to corner. It didn't even touch its sick companion, didn't pay any attention to it at all. It was just careful not to step in its puddle. I tossed it back into the box under the bed. It was glad to be there.

I took the rusty guinea pig out of the cage and carried it off to the bathroom. I examined it. Its tummy was bloated, the skin tight and blue. Of course, we could have cured it if we had done it right off. If I had known that it would have so much stamina of its own, I could have taken it to a veterinarian. But I had thought that guinea pigs would die like flies, unnoticed, insignificantly, and thus certainly painlessly. From now on I won't even know for certain whether the flies don't die tragically and in complex manner.

A spasm shook the guinea pig's tummy. Where is the problem? Its little behind is stopped up. Glued up with dried phlegm mixed with the dust from the hay where the little creature had been sitting and dragging itself back and forth all day in its solitude. I attempted to loosen the scab, gently. The guinea pig, with its eyes so sunken that you couldn't tell they were there, opened its mouth to scream, but not a sound emerged. Wouldn't it be much more merciful to tap its head against the wall? I placed it on the edge of the tub. I turned on the taps of the sink, mixing hot water with cold to make it warm. Apparently in response to the cool enamel surface, the guinea pig scratched shakily, tapped its teeth on the tub and for the last time emitted the first sound it ever made in our household. It was the peep of a bird, the squeak of a child, an unconscious and entirely useless call. There was no one here by that name at all.

I picked the tiny animal up very carefully, moistened the scab, and gently—and painlessly, I hoped—I peeled it off. I expected the pressure to be released and the tummy, so cruelly overfilled, to void itself. But it didn't. It was the last possibility, the last chance. Since this morning when I had played the G-D chord for it in the conviction that it would soon be all over for it, it had lived a full twelve hours. Long enough for penicillin to take effect. Should I tap its head against the tub here and now?

Suddenly the guinea pig began opening its mouth spas-modically, mutely, and something was twitching in its chest. I noticed that the little palms had turned from black to gray since the morning. How could I still help it now, if I really wanted to? I mean, if I were to say that now I would do anything, if it would help him. The guinea pig relaxed again, I thought it was the end but it wasn't. I took another look at his poor little be-hind. The hole was folded into a star shape. It reminded me quite a bit of the dry and wrinkled mouth of Mr. Maelstrom, tightly closed and bluish. I looked over my shoulder at all four walls, I placed my lips to that corpselike orifice and proceeded to suck. To no avail, of course. I didn't even feel the disgust that the circumstances warranted. Then quite sensibly I spat into the sink and rinsed my mouth over and over. I placed the dead guinea pig on the edge of the tub. I was only the calmer for it all.

I went to announce that Red had finally died.

IX

I have a new guinea pig. Its fur is white and its eyes are red. An albino, just like our Albínek, except that it is bigger. Its name is Ruprecht. It's a male. Albínek is almost certainly a female now. So we have a pair of nice, healthy white guinea pigs, Ruprecht and Albínek. Albínek being a boy's name, maybe you'll get a little confused sometimes, children, but that doesn't matter.

How do I know that Ruprecht is a male? I simply told them in the store that I wanted a male. And I picked out one that was older than Albínek, so it would be closer to the final appearance of an adult guinea pig. A guinea pig attains sexual maturity very early, at about six weeks, so our Albínek is mature already that way, but he isn't fully developed yet. He looks about half the size of Ruprecht. And Ruprecht is still growing! According to Pavel, he weighs 510 grammes now, and—according to the books —could weigh up to 800 grammes. According to Vašek, he'll never live to get that big, whereas a kitten would weigh 800 grammes to start with.

We were all very curious about Ruprecht's first response, each of us for vaguely differing reasons. A first response is something entirely different from all other aids to analyzing a personality. The first response is the most revealing. Children! When you get a new guinea pig, no, when you get a new teacher, watch for his first response. Give him a quick once over as he walks in through the classroom door, follow his step to the platform, observe the gesture with which he pushes back his chair, sits down, reaches in his pocket and places his watch on the desk; observe it all and garner your first impressions, but don't launch into any prognoses. Note the cut of his clothes and his hair, the cleanness of his shoes, but don't jump to any conclusions. The angle of his back, the structure of his face, perceive it all, but don't try to explain it; you still can't guess where he is aiming. No, not until you witness his first response, his first deed, do you have the right to a hypothesis. What do we call a deed? The new teacher can say good morning and introduce himself, or else he can give a silent signal to sit down. That's not a deed, just like placing his watch on the desk needn't be a deed. Here, it is hard to advise you, not even I can tell you in all certainty what you can consider a syndromatic phenomenon and what you can consider a phenomenon demonstrating personality. If I say deed, or response, I don't necessarily mean a bang on the desk or a somersault. It might even be that silent gesture indicating that you may be seated, or the knock of the watch on the desk top. In short, a deed or response is an expression of the teacher's presence in the given space that influences further events and relationships in that space. There is certainly a difference if the teacher says, "Get out your textbooks," or if he says, "Clear everything off your desks." I knew a teacher who walked into a classroom through the door, and without stopping, walked right out again through the window. He wasn't a nut, he was just a psychologist. On the basis of who followed him out the window and who stayed behind in the classroom, he could, in his very first hour as a substitute, classify the pupils into clever ones and dumb ones.

Teachers! The same goes for school principals! Observe the first deed of your new principals carefully. Principals! That goes for the initial response of inspectors, too! And finally, even you inspectors! Observe the first deed of your new guinea pig!

When we introduced Ruprecht into the cage, he ran around a few times, apparently surprised that he had to turn so many corners. The cage in the store had been bigger. But that wasn't a deed; that was the environment affecting Ruprecht and not vice versa. His deed follows. When he stumbled over Albínek sitting frozen in a corner, he sniffed his head, and then he wanted to do the same honor to his opposite end, but he couldn't, because it was crammed in the corner. He poked Albínek in the side with his nose, causing the timid thing to squeak and scramble into another corner, where he messed himself. And then Ruprecht emitted a sort of pleasant sound, the like of which we hadn't heard before. It was a gentle murmur something like a cat's purr, but louder. It sounded more like cooing. And at the same time, he showed us something that we had never seen before either. He lifted his rear end on his straddled legs, raised himself up on his toes and began to step from one foot to the other in a very comic manner. He looked like a dandy in jodhpurs who arrives proudly at a ball, but is oblivious of the fact that he left his boots at home. We all laughed, and in addition, Eva was amazed. But above all, our silly little Albínka (we assumed now that Albínek is female) was frightened at the strange visitor who was making himself at home. Ruprecht kept repeating his cooing, rubbing his cheek against her ear, but finally saw that it was a lost cause, and so he turned to other matters: the carrots and the apple He began to eat briskly. While he was eating, he occasionally recalled what he had started out to say, and would give a little coo and a wiggle of his jodhpurs over the carrots, but that was the end of it.

And that was the end of it, for good and ever, never anything that could be described here in a more lascivious fashion, so that Eva and I wondered how Pavel would arrange for those baby guinea pigs of his. Lascivious, if you please, means popular with both ladies and gentlemen.

Now the difference between the two guinea pigs is apparent. While Albínka's face is narrower, Ruprecht's features are cruder, his snout is shorter and less pointy. Albínka's fur is white and delicate like the fur of a white kitten, Ruprecht's is coarser, with an ivory cast, like the yellowish hair on a white goat. Her little ears are fine and delicate and fragile, while his are fresh lugs, sassy, if not brassy. And his entire figure is stronger, more solid, tougher. He jerks his head with greater determination when he is stroked against his wishes. He bit my finger. But he'll never do it again, because I used the same finger to tweak his nose. No, he'll never do it again, but I'm a little sorry: I need another guinea pig so I could observe how a specimen behaves that isn't cuddled and punished.

Why did we get Ruprecht? Did I want to make up to Pavel for the loss of Red? Maybe. But more than that I wanted to find out the extent to which Red's suicidal temperament was a matter of his sex, and the degree to which his personal characteristics were also tied in with his coloring. I was also relying on the fact that if we have a pair, we might get to see it breed. Up till now, the only things I'd ever seen breed were slugs, flies and maybe a hen and a rooster. And finally, I didn't feel like telling my colleague Karásek that we only had one guinea pig. We still have two.

My colleague Karásek! We have been sharing an office for five years and it never occurred to me that we don't know each other. I considered him to be a person who was eccentrically introverted, something that concerned me so little that his introversion didn't budge me, nor did I judge it. I was pleased that he didn't concern himself with me either. I am not much of a talker. Monday mornings, for example, I don't feel the need to exchange descriptions of Sunday afternoons, nor am I curious how the kiddies are doing. I have no compulsion to send my regards to anyone's wife. If I see an acquaintance getting on my train, I make for the furthermost car. Damn, I don't like acquaintances.

In the five years that we have worked together, my colleague Karásek and I have never even walked as far as the trolley car together—not to speak of exchanging invitations for tea. I don't even know where he lives. Before I went to work at the State Bank, I used to be employed in a savings bank, where they cultivated the so-called "socialist life style." They introduced me to it when I was brand new on the job by putting a bouquet of flowers on my desk for decoration, and calling a department meeting (within a compulsory period of fourteen working days after I was hired) where they all got up and recited their autobiographies one after the other, and then I did too. Then my wife and I were invited to tea, and we issued invitations too. A circle of friends began to form, out of which I dropped during our joint vacation. It was like this: At the campfire one evening, an elderly, lyrically inclined lady colleague recited a poem in classical style:

"Don't wonder if some lovely morn/ The birdies sing of thee,/ The other day they came at dawn / To have a look at me. / They came again, and every day / As if a friend to see, / And well they might and well they may / For I am just as free as they, / We sing in the same key."

To this I responded with a complete sentence. It contained words that up until that day I had never spoken aloud. I said: . . . but no, I'm not going to repeat it here, I couldn't, and besides, it doesn't matter any more.

What an immense relief, then, working in a big institution and sharing an office with Mr. Karásek—a decent person who says good morning and makes no more inroads on your private thoughts. Together we turn and flip hundred-crown notes. That's a slim enough basis for friendship. Karásek didn't appeal to me, and apparently I didn't appeal to him much either. The mutual realization of this state of affairs aroused in the two of us, I think, a certain mutual respect, which over the years developed into a certain fondness. And the little bits of maliciousness? Oh, there are lots of people who appear solid and sensible, you see them and respect them, but you don't do any palling around with them because your pallability is limited and you are sure they understand. But stop! You are wrong, because when they drink too much, they trundle over to you uncertainly, embrace you and speak out self-critically:

"I know you don't give a shit about me because I'm stoopid."

"You're wrong, Charlie, I do give a shit about you," you say in a friendly tone, and once again you are surprised at the small number of solid, sensible people in the world who feel completely free towards you, even though you allow so many people the ideal conditions: you pay no attention to them.

If I might give you a bit of advice, boys, don't think about people so much. And when you do, because you have to, think about them in a way that will produce the same results as if you hadn't. Tree grows side by side with tree, and that's that. Let your thinking be a credit and not a burden. And as to you, girls, I am at a loss for words.

Early the day that I bought the new guinea pig, I spoke to my colleague Karásek: "If, when you said you didn't want to talk about a certain matter here, you meant that the conditions in this room weren't favorable to such a conversation, we might take it up elsewhere."

Although a week had elapsed since our conversation about Mr. Maelstrom, he knew right away what I was talking about. He replied: "Unfortunately, friend, the sentence to which you have just given voice has loused up the whole matter entirely, and I don't have a thing to talk to you about any more."

Thus, he gave me a clear answer to my question and also rejected my appeal, but the fault was mine. I should have started out about guinea pigs and we could have gotten together, as before, on account of the guinea pigs. More's the pity.

I considered trying to come to an understanding with Mr. Maelstrom alone. It only meant pulling myself together and sneaking up there to the seventh floor again on my own. No problem there, of course, but I don't really know what to ask if the reply to my first and main question would be incomprehensible. Two people ask more easily than one. I turned to my colleague Karásek again, trying to undo the "more's the pity":

"How are your guinea pigs standing up under your care, friend?"

He raised his heavy red face to mine, moved his mighty jaw for a few seconds, tossed a bundle of bank notes into his desk drawer, slammed the drawer shut and looked at me for a few more seconds. I didn't know what had charged him up like that, but it was apparent even to me that he might explode. All right, this conversation wasn't going to lead to any clandestine encounter for the purpose of showing each other our respective guinea pigs and so forth. He grimaced and replied softly, "The same to you, friend!"

He removed a box of matches and a pack of cigarettes from a different drawer, and left the room. Well, what do you know! And that was when I decided to buy another guinea pig. All I had with me, though, was sixty hellers trolley car fare. I decided to try to collect my bonus today. I picked up a bundle of hundreds, counted out five of them, and after due consideration placed them in my billfold. I left my departure from the bank and my progress past the guards to the inspiration of the moment. Trying to think something up in advance is particularly useless in the State Bank. My departure from the bank and my progress past the guards took place as follows:

I stepped off the paternoster and could see from a distance that the merry search was on. Several bankers were standing there with their arms raised, the contents of their pockets at their feet in piles. One young teller had his pants down to the tiles on the floor and the guard was just fishing in the pocket of his shorts. Women were emerging from a special cabin, hurriedly arranging the straps of their brassieres through their necklines, hurrying to school and preferably away from the guards. The same performance as every day. The doors revolved cheerfully beyond the fortress of the guards. The evil of the unavoidable carried me toward the exit too, and at the last moment, I tried to pick the right guard. On a sudden impulse, I aimed toward a tall fellow with protruding veins, generally known for his vile temper. I noticed that Mr. Maelstrom was just undergoing the frisking, although no one had ever found anything on him. It was assumed that he didn't steal, being unable at his age to adapt to the new ways. But the guards certainly didn't know anything about that, and they wouldn't have cared if they had known. They had just turned the old gentleman's overcoat pockets inside out, and ordered him to remove his right shoe. He went through it all with a calm and resigned air, only his lips moved noiselessly, and he kept glancing at the ceiling, trying to touch his nose with his chin. Then he picked up his briefcase, unbuttoned the strap, revealed the blue canteen, lifted the lid, and was allowed to pass on.

I stepped up to the guard I had selected, and when I saw that his eye was on me, I reached into my breast pocket, took out my billfold and stuck it in his face. That made him mad, so he pushed my hand away and reached under my coat.

"Here you are, buster!" I kept poking my wallet under his nose.

"Go shove it up your ass," he said, running his hands down my shirt.

"There's five bills in there, stupid!" I reported honestly.

"Who are you calling stupid, you jackass!" he exclaimed and punched me in the face.

"You, your old man and your old lady too!" I shouted. It made him just as mad as I expected. With one hand, he grabbed me by what I think was the scruff of my neck and, with the other, what I knew to be the seat of my trousers and turned me toward the exit. He revolved out of the door with me, making a lot of noise in the process, and with a strong, swift kick he shoved me as far away as he could. The wallet flew out of my hand, but one of the passers-by was kind enough to hand it to me. I said thank you and strolled down the boulevard. I was satisfied.

When I got home, everybody was delighted. I left the guinea pig till the end. First I gave Eva a bunch of snowdrops. Then I showed them my new shoes, for ninety crowns. Then I gave each of the boys a chocolate bar. The rest of the money I turned over to Eva. She counted it, and then, happily, gave me ten crowns back, saying that it was for the next day. Only then did I come out with the guinea pig in its box. That was the high point of my surprise.

"Carrooties," called Pavel, "do we have any carrooties at home? Or any patooties?"

"But what if it ups and dies on us again?" asked Eva.

"It isn't going to die," I assured her.

Late that night when I was busy as usual at my figures, and everyone else was asleep, I suddenly realized, strangely disturbed, that I had a guinea pig. A living creature, my own equal. I went to get him. He was heavy, as compared to Albínek, he was silent and confident. When I stood him on the table beside my papers, he waited a while, then began to turn and retreat, and peed on the floor directly under the edge of the table. I'm not sure whether or not I should admire him for that. I dried up the puddle with some newspapers and threw them in the wastebasket. The guinea pig walked around my papers, sniffed them, and took a few nibbles at them. Then it brought its little butt close to the tablecloth and bent over, but it didn't make a puddle. What it made was a brand-new, shiny, oblong black turd. I took a pencil that I had handy and tapped the self-assured little shitter across the butt. He hunched over and rolled his eyes. He wiggled his nostrils and didn't dare do anything else. A few minutes later, he began to raise himself up, but slowly, ever so slowly, millimeter by millimeter. I looked at my watch. When he had picked himself up a little, he tucked his outstretched front leg beneath him carefully, and froze again. And then, almost imperceptibly, he began to straighten up again, stretching his spine into an arc, pulling his tummy in, then he bent over almost imperceptibly to the left, and waited. When nothing happened, he tucked his right front foot—which wasn't supporting much of his weight—closer to his body, and began to raise himself up on it, bit by bit. I looked at my watch. Fifteen minutes. In fifteen minutes he had succeeded in getting his right front paw under his chest. Then he looked about jerkily; he saw me, but I wasn't moving, I was just raising the pencil, bit by bit, almost imperceptibly.

And then all of a sudden the little guy jerked his right foot off the table, pressed it to his chest and straightened up. I raised the pencil a little, and at that the little shitter raised his butt, stuck it forward, and whoops! Like a bolt of lightning he dropped his head, picked up the turd between his teeth, and in a flash had swallowed it.

I dropped the pencil to the table in my surprise. The guinea pig looked around nonchalantly and set out for a stroll. It had every reason to feel satisfied.

X

The air was full of the changes that usually accompany spring. I was possessed with the urge to walk to work, and at the same time to check up on a certain matter. I looked at my watch and then at the public clock on the corner to see if I had enough time. The clock on the corner was twenty minutes slow again, which indicated that our town clocksmith was not on the ball again today. I could rely only on myself. I walked down the block to the next corner, where I came upon the excavation. The same huge pipes were still lying there; somebody had welded them and had gone off to take care of something, something that wasn't too urgent, or else he'd have been back already. My older son was sitting astraddle one of the pipes, but this time I didn't intend to let him fool me.

"Hey, there, boy! Do we know each other?"

The boy looked up and replied, "Hi, Dad. Maybe we do."

"Where's your blue windbreaker?" I asked, squatting over the ditch.

"I don't have one. Mom told you that already."

"Why the hell aren't you in school?"

"I'm going, I'm going," he said, jumped off the pipe and walked alongside it.

"Up here," I called to him.

"It's closer this way," he replied, but he was scrambling up already as he spoke.

"Do you want a slap?" I asked.

"Thanks, but no, thanks, I still have some left over from last time," he replied.

"Where are your things?" I asked.

"In school," he said.

"You've been to school already?" I was surprised.

"Sure I have. I just made a little side trip through the ditch out to here, and now that you're making me go back on the surface, the hall patrol is going to nab me and I'm going to get in trouble."

"Serves you right, you shouldn't have left!" I said. "We'll talk about it when we get home."

I got to the river and decided to walk over the bridge. On the way I wondered whether the pipes led across the river on the bridge or along the river bed. On the bridge. That's clever. The streets were busy. Shouldn't I change jobs?

At the entrance to the State Bank, the guards gave me a slip of paper with the amount of money I had on me when I came in. Okay, so it was ten crowns. They'll write down what I spend in the canteen on the right side. As soon as I walked in, I felt that the atmosphere had changed since the previous day. The crowd at the newsstand was bigger and denser. I found out what was happening from a cheerful colleague Karásek.

"How did you make out yesterday?" he greeted me chummily.

"Great. I walked out with five hundred."

"That's what I call talent. Don't you know what happened?"

"I could tell there was some excitement, but I don't know anything."

He snickered. "Anybody they caught with anything on him, they confiscated everything. Even his own money!"

"But that's . . . that's stealing!" I said.

Nobody had expected events to take that course. It was a clever idea. You can't even go and complain to the authorities:

"When I was carrying home some money from the State Treasury, I was robbed of my own pocket money . . ." Everything goes, no holds barred, it's worse than Chicago.

As we worked, my colleague Karásek and I tried to analyze the new security measures. Was it the idea of the guards? Or was it from higher up? Let us pose the classical question: *Cui bono?* Who will benefit? And let us reply that in conditions like ours, all Latin phrases, mathematical formulae and physical laws are mere prattle, just about as valid as a coin—as a political economist would have said—that has been withdrawn from circulation. Who knows, nowadays, who will benefit from what?

Nor could my colleague Karásek and I agree on what could be expected from the new measure. If they expect it to stop us from stealing, then it must be the work of some consolidationist force within the government, trying to stop the leakage of currency into mysterious circulation. On the other hand, a government force that would want to use the guards for this purpose would have to have control over them, and if it knew how to do that, mysterious circulation would never have come into being. But do they really expect us to stop stealing? They know very well that we are obliged to. My colleague Karásek said that we'd have to wait until the next searches. If they're as tough as these were, then they are obviously aimed at stopping thievery and we can assume that it's a government campaign. I objected that the mere thoroughness of the searches wouldn't tell us anything, if we assume that the currency that we stole is turned in by the guards, whereas the pocket money that is stolen from us is kept by them. By maintaining the same stringency in the searches, the whole thing could just as easily be a government measure as one initiated by the guards themselves or, it could even be half governmental and half guard. On the other hand, if the searches are more relaxed, I said, it would be almost certain that the whole thing was a guard-initiated campaign. Because by relaxing the searches, the guards would try to inspire us to start stealing as much as before, and then jump us and pick up a fortune. My colleague Karásek objected to this assumption of mine by saying that the very process of alternating tough and easy searches would indicate to him personally that it must be a government campaign: the guards would carry it out with a natural apathy, and would only be revived when somebody gets on their backs. I commented—for the second time—that if the government could get on the guards' backs, there wouldn't ever have been anything like mysterious circulation. Then my colleague Karásek said,

"What if it implies changes in the government?"

The only thing I could do in reply to that conjecture was to raise a finger and whistle softly: "Phew!"

"In that case," I added to my whistle, "until the new government raises the salaries of its bankers, many of them, including myself, will have to help themselves any way they can."

"Certainly," my colleague Karásek expressed his solidarity, although he doesn't have any children at home to support any more.

I sighed: "I steal five hundred, they confiscate five hundred and ten. Worse than Chicago!"

My colleague Karásek remarked that we didn't have to bring ten crowns to the bank, and that sixty hellers trolley car fare was plenty. I replied that even that was a loss, and besides, it would mean walking home, unless we stopped bringing any money at all, and left it in the car or whatever.

That's a good laugh. But seriously, now. One way or the other, the new security measures would have an effect similar to that of raising the main prize in a lottery. Like for instance, me, yesterday: if I had known, I would have taken five thousand and not just five hundred . . .

"There, I have it!" my colleague Karásek exclaimed. "It's an anti-governmental campaign on the part of the guards."

How did he arrive at this conclusion? The new measures assume that every banker brings ten crowns from home, but he is going to try to get home with five thousand, if anything. In most cases, they will confiscate all that, so that the influx of currency into the mysterious fund will increase. And so we finally agreed that it is a colossal "undermine" for our state bank. And we feel sorry for it.

A brand-new idea flashed through my mind. "Let's quit stealing," I said.

"For God's sake, how do you ever expect to organize something like that?"

"Not organize, just declare it and do it," I said. "The word will get around."

"How long do you think you could get away with it?" he smiled.

"Personally," I said, "in order to get even with those bastards, I'd be willing not to steal on the side of the government for a long time. One hell of a long time."

"It can't work without some organization. You'll be alone. All alone!"

"So let's organize it."

"That, friend, is something," he said, "that I am not willing to discuss here.'

When I stared at him uncomprehending, he added, "Don't you want us to get together someplace after work and talk about guinea pigs?"

The day flew by with excitement reigning in the corridors of the State Bank and it was almost pleasant. Something appears to be moving, that is what we tell ourselves when our animal optimism instructs us to find something good in events.

At noon, I caught a glimpse of Mr. Maelstrom in the cafeteria. It occurred to me that the entire scholarly debate that I had had with my colleague Karásek was naturally based on Mr. Maelstrom's hypothesis. We are still assuming that there is such a thing as mysterious circulation; we consider everything that happens in reference to it and we attempt to make all the facts concur with the old gentleman's conjecture. But is it justified? And who is familiar, at least, with the conjecture in its entirety?

I picked up my tray and approached the engineer's table.

"Is this seat occupied, sir?" I asked.

He raised a pair of surprised, frightened eyes to my face.

"C-certainly, n-naturally," the old man chattered through his sticky lips.

I sat down and arranged my food. I stirred my soup with a spoon.

"Please forgive me for being so rude as to disturb your lunch . . . "

"Of course, naturally," he urged me on quickly. No one had ever sat down at his table.

"I have something of an interest in classical economy," I began.

"Yes, of course, of course," he chattered again, with a bit of a lisp.

"I looked up the Maelstrom on the maps . . . " I stopped short.

"Oh, no, no, no," he said quickly, "I don't wish to talk about that! Certainly not here, sir."

"Sorry," I said.

"Look me up some time," he managed to say absently, but then he backed down rapidly, "but please, not in the office. Not that! And, if you please, would you kindly excuse me now?"

I understood that I was the one who should kindly excuse himself. With a bow, incapable of saying a single word, I picked up my tray and wove my way to the other side of the dining room. Everyone was watching. I picked a table where I would be alone. Would that stick with me?

Later, between afternoon and evening, when it is still daylight on the street but the lights in banks and offices are on already, when the waxed floorboards dating back to the days of lombard creak under the heavy, weary feet of departing bankers, when brooms and mops and buckets are rubbing their eyes and stretching their limbs in preparation for their own shift—in short, later on that day, I got on the paternoster and rode up to the seventh floor. I creaked down the narrow corridor under the white electric spheres to a certain door with a key in it. The metal oval with the number 706 embossed on it was still swinging back and forth as it dangled from the key ring. Had he just left, or just arrived? I knocked feebly on the door, and without waiting, walked in. Inside the room, there was no one.

Just like the last time, the heavy old-fashioned desk with its railing, the inkwell and the semicircular rocker with its blotting paper. A key was stuck in the desk drawer, one of a bunch that was also still swinging back and forth. The wardrobe to my right, the bare wall to my left. Behind the desk, hidden, was a barrel, as you recall. I knocked on it, it was empty. I couldn't see any opening anyplace where something could be poured, stuffed or put into it. I walked over to the wardrobe and opened it with a loud creak. The engineer's gray coat and black hat, no papers, not even a single paper. Only the blue canteen stood on the floor, the familiar blue canteen. Something seemed wrong with its standing here. Now, after lunch, it ought to be in the cold behind the window. Or was it empty today? I picked it up, it was heavy. I lifted the lid. The unpleasant sourish smell of soup. Sorry, more's the pity! I sloshed the wide-mouthed canteen around a little, the paprika rusty layer of grease rolled back, uncovering a fluid with noodles swimming about in it. But at the same time, I felt something heavier rolling around at the bottom of the canteen. I think you know what it was, children . . . I had sensed it as soon as I saw the canteen standing in the wardrobe.

That day leaving the bank was once again full of suspense. Bankers all, we walked towards the cordon of our old acquaintances fully aware of the fact that we would learn more today than we knew yesterday. One good thing about these cops of ours is that every day put on a fresh expression of indifference; they don't tie in with what happened the previous day, not with anybody. I could approach my benefactor of the previous day with the certainty that he would treat me according to his will today, without the slightest trace of his will yesterday. Nothing would be there to indicate that yesterday we had slugged each other. So I headed toward him again. He let me through without a search. He waved a hand. Fool that I am! Five thousand down the drain.

I left the State Bank and found myself in a group of bankers who were waiting to find out how their other colleagues had managed. But nobody fell on the sidewalk the way I had the day before. For the present, it looked, for all the world, as if the guards were checking carefully, but only at random. My colleague Karásek was waiting for me at the corner.

"So what are we to think about it all, friend?" I asked.

"Nothing," he replied. "We'll just wait."

We walked down the boulevard. Talking was difficult, people

kept bumping into us. We crossed the street and went through a courtyard into the Franciscan Garden. There, I said, "What shall we decide on?"

"Like, about what?" he asked, and hurried on alongside me.

"I mean what we will do from now on," I said, surprised that he no longer knew why we had agreed to meet.

We came to a side path, away from the streetlights. My colleague Karásek stopped short. I couldn't see his face, but I could tell that he was trying to make up his mind whether or not to confide in me.

"For the present, what we'll do," he said, "is that as of this moment you will stop snooping around in the old gentleman's office. And if you don't, I'll pay you off in ready bills, like this!" and he punched me with his fist in the stomach.

At home.

"Dad, you said that we were going to talk something over," Vašek started at supper time.

"What's there to talk over? I don't know."

"How should I know. You're the one that said it."

"What was it about?"

"Probably me. Or else the pipes," he snickered.

"What have pipes got to do with you?" I asked.

"He lies around with them in the ditch," giggled Pavel.

"When was I supposed to have said that?" I asked.

"This morning, I suppose." Vašek was surprised.

"Why did I say it?"

"Because I made you mad, I guess."

"You didn't make me mad. Now you're making me mad."

"You two remind me of Spejbl and Hurvínek," said Eva.

"I can draw a picture for you if you want me to. But when do you want to see it?" said Vašek.

"See what? What are you supposed to draw me a picture of, for pity's sake?"

"The network of canals, like you told me. But I only know it on this side of the river."

"And is this side connected with the other side somehow?" I asked.

"I'd have to look into that."

"And when did we discuss it? Today?"

"This morning. When we saw each other this morning."

"And how come you left your classroom? Tell me that! Aha!"

"She told us what pages to read and then she went away," Vašek replied.

"She! Who is she?" said Eva.

"Her? probably his stupid teacher," I said.

"You think everybody is stupid," said Eva, "except you. And you can't remember things from morning till evening."

"What was I supposed to have remembered from this morning?" I asked, raising my voice.

The boys started to laugh, Pavel out loud, Vašek a little more softly.

"What did you tell me to remember this morning?" I shouted, and got up from the table. "And what do you want me to remember tomorrow? Speak clearly and distinctly. I promise I'll take it to heart!"

Vašek wasn't laughing any more, his face had frozen. Pavel didn't want to laugh any more either, but his nose started running, and he had to.

I slammed the door and walked away from the house.

XI

Sunday came. It came with a white sky which occasionally emitted a delicate, icy flake of snow. The air still smelled of the cold but it wasn't weather for any serious freezing. The sparrows were yelling in the eaves, the seagulls by the river, while in the parks, the blackbirds exchanged brief comments on life in general. This year's mild winter hadn't brought much snow, and what was left of it had thawed within the last few warm days, so that there was a threat of the imminent outbreak of forsythia blossoms. Last night, the night that opened onto Sunday, brought a light frost which might slow things down a little, and that's fine. An early spring is usually muddy, unpleasant, misleading; mud everywhere, the flu virus, waiting for spring which won't come for a while yet, and finally, fatigue, spring fever. It is best when winter takes out everything that it has coming to it and then really goes to the devil. And so I really enjoy this kind of a cold Sunday, and getting up and going out for a solitary walk toward the old merry-go-round that wasn't going round yet, all alone except for the guinea pig in the pocket of my overcoat. I looked up at the sky with its translucent mask; behind it, the sun was grinding the frosty

91

stratosphere into white flakes, and I said to myself, I'm going to declare a family outing.

Quick decisions, that's the best kind. Little things and unimportant decisions can only be right when they are made instantly. Listen, girls! When you grow up and go pick yourself a husband take note and test him! If you find someone who hasn't got the gumption to make a minor and insignificant decision instantly—even if possibly wrongly—you can't expect him to make a solid, well-thought-out and thoroughly considered decision on matters of importance and consequence. Listen, boys and youths! When you select yourself a wife reject all applicants who can't accept your instant decisions—important or unimportant, right or wrong—with at least a sense of humor.

Eva, for example, was chosen well, even though the one who made the choice considered things for long and slowly. So that my instant decisions don't bother her; she would just like to know about them "a few days in advance." If she is presented with them only an hour in advance, though, it doesn't matter either, if the whole thing turns out well. The point is, the whole thing doesn't turn out well if Eva doesn't care for the idea from the outset, and the best thing to do then is to drop it right off after a short argument.

"Get ready, everybody, we're going for an outing," I announced merrily in the hall.

"So I'll fix lunch for supper," said Eva pensively, looking out the window, "and now I'll just put something between some bread. Salami. But what'll we wear?"

"I'll wear those old trousers," said Vašek willingly.

"And the blue windbreaker," I added.

The water in the toilet gurgled. Pavel came out, walked over to the sink and said enthusiastically, "Dad, did you say we were going to go for a hike or a trip?"

"Yes," I said. And added, "If you kept office hours like civilized people, you would have been out of there by the time I said it, and you'd have heard what I said."

"A trip," said Eva.

"Wow!" commented Pavel softly.

"Our train leaves the Smíchov Station at ten o'clock." I added.

"That means we're going to have to leave the house by a quarter past ten," said Vašek.

"Are you stupid or something?" Pavel turned on him.

"Don't splash water on my nice clean floor," Eva said angrily.

"Dry your hands!" I told him.

Eva started to get the boys ready. In the children's room, she said, "Where's the other guinea pig?"

"What do you mean?" asked Pavel. "Did you put it somewere else, Vašek?"

"Not me," said Vašek. "Didn't you forget it in bed from last night?"

"No," he replied, "I put it back in the cage last night."

"Aha!" I said, and he caught one behind the ear. "Guinea pigs don't belong in bed."

Then I went out into the hall, took the guinea pig out of my overcoat pocket, and without anyone noticing, I stuck it inside Pavel's pillow case.

"Here it is. See? Again." I said.

"That's funny. Now I don't understand that at all," said Pavel, astonished.

"There are a lot of things I don't understand in life, either, pal," I said.

It was ten o'clock; the elected train must be pulling out of the station already, and there we were, just catching a trolley bus.

"Maybe there's another one," whined Pavel.

"Sure," said Vašek briefly. "Sure."

"Then maybe we can take that one," said Pavel.

"We cannot," I said. "Shoes are supposed to get shined on Saturday."

"But if I forgot to shine them yesterday and I didn't shine them till today, and so we missed the ten o'clock, we could catch the next train, couldn't we? Huh?"

"We can't," said Vašek shortly. "Shoes get shined Saturdays."

"And as for you, Vašek," said Eva, "you had better pipe down and don't irritate your father."

We passed the railroad station. Vašek turned the other way coldly, while Pavel raged under his breath. We got off at the last stop and walked through the deserted square. The air was pleasant, cool and windless, plenty of time and nothing to do, the kids were fine, the food was in the knapsack and nobody to care about us one way or the other.

"Whoever is good will be richly rewarded," I said.

"I wonder," said Pavel.

Vašek was dragging his feet a little further on, mumbling to himself, " . . . richly rewarded, richly rewarded . . . "

We walked along the brook, down the valley that we all knew, but we hadn't been there for a long time, and we had never been there this time of the year. We looked at the houses and gardens of the people who, for the most part were still in bed. We saw the rag-wrapped and whitewashed trunks of apple trees and the garden plots insulated by evergreen branches. We examined garden walls and fences and gates with bells on them; we read the names of the inhabitants. How did the fellow with his name on the gate get this far, by what kind of thievery, and where is he going from here, and what is his wife cooking for lunch and what about their dog and their cat? And what about our guinea pigs? No grass to be found anywhere. Would a guinea pig eat an evergreen twig? It's just as green and fresh. Chlorophyll is good for guinea pigs and birds. Vitamins and tannin. Essences and resins.

"Eva!"

"What?"

"Nothing."

"What are you two talking about?" Pavel wondered.

"You keep out of it," said Vašek.

And so we came to the place where the viaducts carrying the tracks of two railroad lines intertwine over the Hlubočepy Valley. A mind-boggling view for the boys. I must say that mine boggled at the sight of it too, the cool gray of the stone pillars and arches.

"Here's your reward, gentlemen!" I declared.

"Great, Dad. Wow!" nodded Vašek. "You really pulled one off this time."

"You really pulled one off this time, Dad," said Pavel. "And where did you get all the material?"

There is a brook running under the viaduct. And a path running alongside it. Bordering the path are little cottages, vestiges of long-gone neighborly days. They are kept in such good repair that it is touching. Resting by the bank of the brook, with stone stairs leading down to the water, under the old stone viaducts, the cottages are a truly picturesque sight, or pretty like a picture. Whenever Eva sees a sight like that, she wishes she could move away from all the fame and glory that is Prague, into a cottage like that, plant some bulbs and wait to find out what comes up. She pointed to a little white cottage just beyond the viaduct. Its roof was red, there was a garden plot under the windows, a picket fence around it. A gate. It was locked. A walk led from the gate to the back of the house where the front door was. There, in the yard at the base of the cliff, that is where I'd build myself a workshop. But what would I do there? I wouldn't do computations. Study, paint, make furniture, bind books? But what would we live on?

"I'd keep chickens. And I'd quit teaching."

"No cow?"

"No cow."

We examined the cottage, the home and property of some laborer or trolley car conductor who carries a briefcase to work, a briefcase with a canteen in it.

"If you look carefully," said Eva, "it seems that this cottage is more neglected than the rest."

"Maybe it's up for sale," I said.

"Go ask that man," said Vašek, nodding at the window where a gray head was visible.

"Would you lend us the money?" asked Eva.

"You can take some at your bank, Dad." Pavel suggested.

The bank again. When I was a boy, the word "bank" used to conjure up images of something as solid as a "B" and as elegant as an "S". A dignified institution, which backs its own reputation on that of others. Currency issues, drafts, obligations, checks, stocks and coupons, promissory notes. And broker and bankruptcy too. Counterfeiting is punishable by law. Loans, mortgages, lombard. Circulation. He told me, Mr. Maelstrom, the commercial engineer, that I should look him up some day, but not at the bank. Where then? How do I know where he lives? And my colleague Karásek told me not to look the old man up. Will I or won't I? I wonder. Naturally, my clever young readers, I realized—as you did—that there is some sort of relationship between those two. What kind of mystery have we here? If, loved ones, I were to examine and study it seriously—and that goes for you too—I would of course solve the mystery, alone and unassisted. By the sheer power of concentration, each and every mystery! I wouldn't even have to ask the old fart what should be done to avoid the depression that is imminent. I am convinced that anyone who meditates can discover certain ideas. In fact, I even found one of the ideas that you propounded, old man, to be fallacious.

You said, didn't you, that if too many banknotes were to disappear from our bank, irretrievably, our bank would have to lay off some of the bankers. Ah, sir! The less currency there is in circulation, the faster it will have to circulate, the more operations per unit of time we will have to carry out on it. In order that the money move faster, we may even have to deliver it in person to the factories, wait there till the workers get paid, run alongside them to the shops, the newsstands, the bars and the movie theatres, get on the managers' backs to fill out the postal receipts, accompany them—or maybe take the money ourselves—to the post-office, and from the post office to our bank . . . In other words, the less currency there is, the more employees will have to service it, until the decreasing number of banknotes and the increasing number of bankers meet and conjugate. Until finally, in a certain sense, all the people in Czechoslovakia become, in a certain way, bankers, friend, and all of Czechoslovakia becomes one great surprising bank.

We left the valley and climbed on the ledge above it. From there, Prague looked like an uncertain conglomerate of form, smoke and glimmer. The sun emerged. We were alone—there wasn't a soul in the fields but us. The afternoon was beginning.

96

The only living things were the hares and the mice that had survived the winter. The sun was shining. We had our lunch. We broke a twig of fir off for our guinea pigs. Forty years in this world. Fifteen of them in Prague, and there it is in the background, unclear, alien and unreachable, we only have each other, and if Prague were to vanish in a pillar of fire, now, this instant, we would be saved, along with everything that matters, except for the guinea pigs.

Eva was staring pensively into the distance, maybe she was thinking about her school, which isn't a game to her. Eva sometimes has weighty thoughts, and I don't know how to lighten them for her.

"You'd have to get to be the principal yourself, so you wouldn't have to listen to a stupid principal," I said.

"And what then?" she asked.

"Then things would repeat themselves," I admitted.

"Where would a person have to end up? Keep going up and up, until that's all that his work would mean to him," she said.

"What about your grum little pupil?" I asked.

"She's home, sick now. And I find teaching easier now that she isn't there."

"Maybe she's the one that will die. Isn't she going to die?" I asked.

"Don't talk like that!" she snapped. "Just so you don't end up the worse for it."

"You'd have to end up the worse for it, because you find teaching easier when she isn't there."

In the meantime, the boys were crawling up the cliffs and caves. Eva and I were sitting in a dip in the sandstone, dry and sheltered from the wind. The sun was shining harder now, and any minute the ants might start climbing out of the ground. I wished they would. Suddenly, I heard a yell. I jumped up, but it wasn't anything, just Pavel who had gotten his shoe jammed in a crack in the cliff and couldn't pull it out. When I reached him, his shoe suddenly came free, all by itself somehow. But he got his ears boxed anyway, and I added, "Don't ever call for help so revoltingly."

"How's he supposed to call for help?" asked Vašek.

"Any old way," I said, "as long as it doesn't disgust his rescuers. That's obvious, idiots."

Eva, her face a pale green, was standing beside me, shaking her head.

"Why did he have to scream like the damned in hell?" I asked her.

"He was frightened."

"He shouldn't get frightened if he knows what's the matter."

"I wasn't frightened," objected Pavel, "it just hurt."

"Serves you right," I said, "because you shouldn't be so clumsy."

"I was just following Vašek."

"Naturally," said Eva, "and Vašek, does he really have to spend all day scrambling up and down cliffs?"

"But . . . But these here aren't even cliffs," Vašek babbled, "besides, there's nowhere to fall here, and can I help it if he . . ."

"You told me to bring you the magnifying glass."

"I know, but that doesn't mean you've got to go and stick your foot . . ."

I turned away and walked on ahead. They kept talking about it for a while, and I asked them to forget about it; they kept on discussing it, I said that they should quit it, immediately. They didn't.

"All right!" I roared. "Now you," I turned to Pavel, "you walk twenty yards ahead of us, and you," I pointed to Vašek, "twenty yards behind. And make it snappy!"

Pavel walked on ahead with a demonstrative limp, because Vašek had asked him to bring him the magnifying glass, but so what? Let him limp. All this while Vašek grumbled angrily behind us, "Beat him up, that's what I'm going to have to do. I end up taking the blame. Dumb cluck, clucking rotten guinea pig, that's what he is!"

He overtook us, grabbed Pavel by the shoulder, gave him a couple of shakes, and when Pavel began to pound him furiously on the chest, he shook him three more times and fell back to where he had been told to walk, behind us. As he passed us on the way back, he said, "Good afternoon. Thank you."

Eva shook her head. I said, "Don't thank us, just be grateful if evening comes without your having gotten walloped!"

"I don't know how I'd come by a walloping, if I'm careful."

"Never mind," I turned back to him, "all you need to do is to be so defensive so soon after the affair of the blue windbreaker."

So he fell silent, and Eva said, "But he doesn't have any blue windbreaker."

"But the affair of the blue windbreaker, he did have that," I said.

We crossed the plateau and came up to the railroad track in the field. We followed it to the whistle stop, which we examined in detail. The coltsfoot on the embankment wasn't in blossom yet. The train schedule pasted up on the wall of the wooden shed told us that a train to Prague would be passing through in twenty minutes. Eva didn't know in which direction it would be going, even though we had just arrived from there, and even though an arrow pointed that way on a sign that read TO PRAGUE. The boys explained it to her, while I took advantage of the peace and quiet to think about any number of things.

Vašek and Pavel were expecting a fine locomotive to pass through here, all stiff and creaky and greasy. Pavel had the audacity to suggest, "What if we waited for the train, Dad, and took it into Prague?"

"Shoes are supposed to get shined on Saturday," Vašek interjected.

"We'll wait for the train," I said, and looked at Vašek. "But we won't ride it to Prague because Vašek doesn't approve."

"Gosh, I didn't mean—that's too bad," said Vašek, and Pavel declared reproachfully, "See?"

But the train that finally appeared, after several warning toots before it rounded the bend, was so beautiful, so spacious and so empty that I was obliged to say, "Okay, all aboard, ladies and gentlemen!"

With a hop, a skip and a thump, the boys were inside. I helped Eva up the high steps, and the train took off. It slid down the hill, it leaned gracefully out of the curves. The boys took a seat on the left side of the train so they could see Prague through the hills, an unusual sight, a dramatic view, while Eva and I sat down beside the boys. But when the train approached the viaduct, I told Eva that we should move to the other side.

"You want to get a bird's eye view of our cottage?" she asked.

The terrain was sloping lower and lower, and we were on a high embankment over the valley. Before the train got onto the viaduct, we caught a short glimpse of the cottage under the hillside. An old man had just emerged from the cottage into the yard as we rode past. He stopped on the threshold, and looked up at the train for an instant. I could have been mistaken, but hardly.

It was Mister Maelstrom.

And guinea pigs—because this book my dears, is about guinea pigs—guinea pigs don't care for evergreens.

XII

I feel like sleeping, terribly, but I can't. I would like to sleep, but I mustn't. I still have my figures to finish up. I get up from the table once in a while and walk around, to help keep awake. I get up from my chair and move my feet to wake myself up. I look out the window—all the windows in the house across the street are dark. Sound asleep! And then I sit down again and concentrate. The hardest sum that brings you past ten is seven and four, the easiest one is nine and eleven. If I poke my eye out with a pencil, that's what the guard is waiting for. Children dear! Spraddle your legs, kiddies, and I'll tell you a story. Did you ever kill anything bigger than a . . . ?

What am I talking about? When you're half asleep, absurd sentences get tangled in your thoughts. I'd better take another walk! Or should I just put away my papers? But there are certain circumstances . . . it's not something you can tell, it's something you've got to figure out, except that I don't know enough to know how. What do I know enough to know how to do? I don't know addition, either, or abstraction. The only thing I how now is—I now how is—I know now is how to put my head down and snore.

I'll go get me a guinea pig. That ought to wake me up and clear my head.

The windows across the street are all dark, but then I have already recorded that fact, why, even my own wife Eva is asleep in its bed, I mean in her head, and our boys are asleep too, in the rabbit hutch. Only the guinea pigs are always half awake. The boys are asleep, but the air in here smells like a rabbit hutch. Yet if I open the door to the balcony, the guinea pigs' cage will be in the draft, down near the floor. The little creatures sleep cuddled up together in the corner, fully dressed. Bare skin is unhealthy, you might say. Why do even black people have hairless skin, if they didn't have to wear so many clothes? But they apparently had to, which means they originated elsewhere. Is that evidence for the case of the monophyletics? But define monophyletics! "When he's asleep, he doesn't even ask for bread"—that's a saying I used to hear as a boy when bread was still something one talked about. That means that during his working hours, he isn't very good at all. Our boys—are they good, or aren't they? I think they are. But I'm not of those parents who habitually and thoughtlessly complain about their kids. They complain, but they don't do anything about them, which becomes clear when you ask a question in passing the next time you meet them. Try asking your friends then. "Well, have you finally beaten some of the sass out of your kids that had you so upset the last time I saw you?" But never mind children. They're by far the lesser evil. Maybe that's even why I am comparatively fond of them.

Being fond of children is an attribute called for in any honorable man. It is evidence of his sensitivity, his fundamental good character, or at least of his good upbringing. Not being fond of kids can even be considered dangerous. Still, I suspect that most people don't really know whether they are fond of children— children in general. Do you like the mountains? *Aimez-vous Brahms?* Those are questions that can be answered freely. Do you like Germans? That's a little harder. And do you like children? Hm, why do you ask? You'll never get off unnoticed with a negative reply. Love of children? What do they mean by that, actually?

As far as I'm concerned, the man I'd view with approval, the man I'd take to dinner, would be the one who would ask me (all of his own accord, and not after reading it here) the only telling question: "What kind of children do you like?"—I don't like pushy, noisy, chattering children. I waste no love on children of parents who consider their children to be of exceptional significance, who require extra good food for their children and who would like their children to be spared all the evils that the rest of us have to live with. I am repelled by children of parents whose children are supposed to live better lives than their parents did, because, why? What for? You exceptional youngsters, rid us of our harassers and then we will have respect for you. Thus it is written, and if it isn't, I just wrote it. Also, I am disgusted by children of parents who are so weak that they can't keep their children under control. If a directive were to be issued saying that everyone has to hold some public office, there is one office that I'd be willing to accept even under the current regime: I'd walk the streets looking for wailing brats who are stupid by origin, and turn them over my knee and whale the tar out of them, to stop the poor wittle darlings fwom cwying. Yes, there are exceptional cases, but I mean really exceptional ones, where the kid can't help himself. But even in cases like that, I don't think that he should have any advantages we don't have. If you can't help crying, you little whelp, here's a whack in the ass to teach you it doesn't pay to holler.

I'll bypass sick and feeble-minded children without a word. But you asked me what kind of children I like. Well, I don't like children of parents who neglected their offspring by not recognizing his talents, turning him into a mild, dull and useless child—a human being that is evil, small and base—an envious, jealous and opportunistic person—in a word, an ass, a dolt, a beast and a whore. Youngsters like that make me sick, and I see them as a threat. When I encounter a stupid child, I wonder that there is such a thing. Have you ever seen a stupid young squirrel in the forest? None of us likes adult lamebrains and blockheads, but little nitwits and numbskulls slip freely among us under the guise of childhood, taking advantage of our tendency to be kind to anything small, accepting our love and goodness, our patience

103

and indulgence, our devotion and geniality. And yet they are the ones who—upon attaining adulthood—will beat anything good out of everybody. It will be their shoes that will kick patience in the butt, theirs will be the fists that will punch placability in the teeth. I can believe that a subnormally clever animal cannot achieve a position of leadership within its pack or herd. But I can't believe that stupid people will be kicked out of their influential positions. I am amazed. First we try, humanely, to rear them to the idea of equality, and they—having achieved power—flatten everything out down to their own level. Such monstrous incompetence on our part cries to heaven. And heaven is really functioning. Try reaching inside the manger at Christmas time.

The guinea pigs that I brought in here are running around all over the couch, clucking. First runs Ruprecht, and behind him Albínka, with her jerky gait and her reproaches as to the length of the track. She always stops just behind him, so that at least her whiskers would be touching him. When she is on alien soil, she prefers to crawl under his neck, with his vigilant head raised and his rear splatted on the floor, a ludicrous sphynx with legs like an old iron stove. The guinea pigs seek refuge under a pillow, because there are buzzards, weasels and hawks circling overhead. They wait until the birds and beasts of prey crawl away before they start to jump around and play tag. They feel free on the couch. It's green, soft underfoot, and warm. But on the table, directly under the light, on the yellow tablecloth, their movements are uneasy and restless. And on top of the wardrobe they hardly stir. They only move to the point of getting close, and then they sit side by side, looking around fearfully. On the glass surface of the coffee table, they don't even stir far enough to get close together; each one sits by itself, quivering. I don't even put the piglets on the floor any more, I don't feel like forever bending over and scraping them out of the crannies between the furniture and the wall.

Up till today, I have not succeeded in attracting one or the other of the guinea pigs on to the palm of my hand. Like one day I closed in Ruprecht in the cold between the inner and the outer windows, figuring that after five minutes, he'd be more than

104

happy to get out of there, even if it meant climbing onto my hand. I was mistaken. When I opened the window, he just sat there, and I had to remove him so he wouldn't get a cold and dysentery together, all at once. It is sad, and it's getting a little dull. Even a mouse has more spirit of adventure, a rat goes so far as to be aggressive, and even clever, under pressure, or so I read somewhere.

You may make a note of this: This period of time a guinea pig needs to pull itself together, or to come to its senses, is fifteen minutes. That is the length of time it takes for a guinea pig to make its first move after being removed from a pleasant to an unpleasant environment. It is not permissible to interrupt this time period. If, for example, you poke the guinea pig with an impatient forefinger and move it a little, it begins to count its fifteen minutes all over again. If you wait patiently for the first exploratory move on the part of the guinea pig, and then, say, all you do is take and turn it around a hundred and eighty degrees, so that its head is where its butt was, bang! And there goes another fifteen minutes. This kind of experiment will cost you a lot of hours of sleep. For a long time there, I couldn't bring a basic and simple experiment to an end: finding out how a guinea pig would handle the situation when it finds itself on a plane surface measuring one by four feet, where there is no plant life and where it is impossible to burrow into the ground due to the fact that it is a bookshelf. This experiment always failed because I moved and the guinea pig was startled and it jumped and began counting all over again, or else, I lost my temper and moved it across the bookshelf myself, or again, somebody interrupted us, or the guinea pig wet itself and I had to clean it up. This was the pattern until one night I finally succeeded in concluding the experiment, and here are the results, for your information: Upon determining that the surface on which it finds itself is limited and finite, a surface from which it is incapable of escaping under its own power, and on which there is nowhere to hide, it squats in place and doesn't do a thing. It just sits and stares, not fifteen minutes but a hundred and fifty or more. It might scratch its belly, it might run its paws across its face, it might doze off; then it wriggles uneasily and emits a turd, and ends up just waiting for the outcome of its experiment with me. And here are the results, also for your information: I pick up the guinea pig, and carry it off to its cage as is my duty, because I am capable of so doing.

Not so the tom-kitten that we used to have; he always wanted to resolve any situation he found himself in. When placed on the top edge of an open door, he would try to keep his balance, almost fall, save himself at the last moment and scramble back up, until he discovered that it would be better to jump than to fall. He jumped, and nothing happened to him. When placed on the chandelier, he would meow at me and keep a narrowed eye on me until I came closer, and then he would jump on my head, carefully, so nothing would happen to either of us.

"A guinea pig is stupid," I said to Pavel this morning.

"Don't talk like that," said Pavel woefully.

"Why not? A guinea pig is stupid, you have to be aware of that," I said.

"A guinea pig isn't stupid," said Vašek. "It is smart enough."

"Can you name me an animal that is any smarter than a guinea pig?" asked Pavel.

"I can. A cow." I said.

"And what makes you think that a cow is more intelligent?" asked Vašek.

But at the moment I have realized that my instant decision happened to turn out wrong: that a cow isn't probably any more intelligent than a guinea pig. I imagined a cow's behavior when faced with various tasks—except that nobody would ever think of facing a cow with various tasks; everybody accepts a cow the way it is.

"You're probably right," I told Vašek.

I have a map, I got hold of a map, Vašek drew me a map of subterranean passages, tunnels, canals and pipes. But I still take the surface route to and from the bank. It's probably just as far, only faster and cleaner that way. The State Band! How do you treat a person who punches you in the stomach with his fist till you fall down, and the next day sits across from you, without explaining a thing, with the most natural expression on his face, until you

106

wonder whether it really happened or not. I do my work and simply don't converse with my colleague Mr. Karásek.

When I place a pillow on the guinea pig, he doesn't run away, no, he just sits there under the pillow. The earth has finally had the kindness to enfold him. He is hidden and enveloped, and as far as all the beasts of prey are concerned, he has vanished, and he is all his own. What a lovely solution, the kind I crave in my dreams of horror. Like when I dreamed that a little girl was running toward me, and throwing her arms around my waist, giggling voicelessly and moving her lips without a sound, pulling me someplace all the while; her little head is massive and pale, and where is it that she is forcing me?—into a barrel, to climb inside a barrel. First she crawls in there herself, and scrooches down, and I'm supposed to scrooch down myself, down to her dubious fragile flesh, because it turns out just then that the little girl is naked. Or else they are shooting at me. But fortunately I don't have that kind of dream very often. I never have one when I sleep in Eva's bed.

When placed in front of a mirror, a guinea pig does not respond to its reflection. I put it on top of the radio and turned on some loud music under it. It didn't pay any attention to that either, even though its hearing is acute. It can tell who is coming by the sound of his footsteps. When it is Eva, the guinea pigs begin to squeal and they put their front feet on the wire mesh, because who is the one that usually feeds them? Eva. I think that their vision is pretty good too, but I still don't know how far they can see. Their sense of smell is very fine and delicate, it wasn't nice of me to put perfume on Ruprecht's forehead. I wanted to see what Albínka would do. She fled from him, she didn't even want to sit next to him. She wasn't even capable of "gnewing" the same carrot as he; she grabbed it and dragged it away, with him behind her, and she trying to get away from him. He couldn't get away from the smell himself. He kept sticking his head under the paper on the floor of the cage and burying it in the wood shavings. Besides, it wasn't a very scientific experiment. What would have been more effective was to have put the perfume on his foot, because he could have tried to do something about it, like trying to "gnew" it off or clean it off, or dragging it behind him on the sidewalk. But what could he do with his forehead. Well, next time.

Take a paper bag, place it open on a table and let the guinea pig crawl inside. Then twist the bag shut, just so the air can get in, and go to the movies. When you get back, you'll find everything just the way it was when you left. Take a glass, fill it with water, then change your mind and pour the water out, and take the glass and turn it upside down over the guinea pig. You can observe the guinea pig through the glass walls, watch it sit there in astonishment, its nostrils quivering with excitement, its tummy undulating nervously, and yet it doesn't even try to determine the penetrability of the wall around it, at least not during the first hour. Let me know, for my information, what happens during the hours that follow.

Take some sticky paper tape and make a ring big enough to slide easily around the guinea pig's neck; slide it there, and wait. When the guinea pig makes its first move, that is, in fifteen minutes, it will feel that it probably has something around its neck. It will shake its head, in an effort to back out of the embracing sensation, then it will scratch the itchy place with its foot, accidentally tearing the tape and freezing itself. Take another piece of paper tape and put it around the guinea pig's body about halfway down, loosely, so that it just barely gathers in the fur. The guinea pig will freeze. It is completely convinced that its hands and feet are tied and it never discovers that they aren't because it doesn't even make an effort to move. I added another piece of tape, around its neck, like a collar. The fur in front of the ring pulled out and stood on spiny end. The silhouette of the familiar guinea pig was entirely transformed. In profile it looked like a ridiculous Prezewalsky horse, or tarpan, while its front view is reminiscent of a dreadful lion that has just devoured a missionary, and inherited the saintly expression on his face. And when just for the hell of it, I pasted a piece of tape on the guinea pig's ears, the unfortunate little creature broke me up entirely.

Don't bother to put a guinea pig on a piano keyboard and close the lid. Again, a guinea pig isn't a kitten: it doesn't play.

108

The guinea pigs that were still running around on the couch a little while ago finally found a hiding place under a little velvet cushion. I wait, watching the motionless cushion, considering, and then all of a sudden I lift it. Aha! Two lovely animals blissfully nestling together, cheek to cheek as if they were in bed. Eyes and whiskers. Who's to stop me?

I scooped them up and placed them on my chest. Alarmed, they climbed over each other, stepping on each other's ears. Each of them tried to burrow into me, and it wouldn't have minded in the least if it had knocked the other one to the ground. But I held them and protected them both. I sat down at the table. I kept Ruprecht in the crook of my arm, and stood Albínka on the table. She took off across the tablecloth, sniffing the terrain, now and then giving a squeak. Ruprecht, who couldn't see her and could only hear her, responded in grumbles, but he didn't go anywhere in search of her. Albínka did the rounds of the table and came back to my side. I leaned an open palm against the edge of the table. She stood by my hand, whining like a witch.

"Come on, sweetie," I said softly.

She began to whine even more, shifti. g her weight from one side to the other.

"Come on, now, sweetheart, come here, don't be afraid!"

She came closer and placed one front paw on my palm.

"Come on, sweetie, don't be afraid, come on!"

Hesitantly, she walked onto my palm as if it were a log bridge; she crossed the abyss, ran up my arm and squeezed into the bend of my elbow. I patted her and carried her off to the cage. In the meantime, I left Ruprecht on the table. I knew what I was going to do about him.

I walked over to the radio and pressed the button that said *Phonograph*. I turned off the speaker and locked the pickup arm. Then I went back to the table where Ruprecht was waiting. I carried him over to the phonograph and wondered what speed I should choose for him. First I tried thirty-three rpm. He huddled down on the turntable and made jerky movements with his head, but otherwise he didn't show any distinct attitude towards what was going on. In his voluntary helplessness, he was incapable of moving closer to the center of the revolving turntable, so that he might keep his nose from bumping against the rim of the phonograph. I was beginning to get mad at him. I stopped the motor and changed the speed to seventy-six. But that was senseless; at that speed Ruprecht was swept off the turntable and he fell behind the pickup. It turned out that forty-five was the best speed. It wasn't enough to make Ruprecht go flying, but it was fast enough to make him show some desire to be left alone. He tried to creep off the speeding turntable, but as soon as he touched something stable he flipped over and began to roll all over the disk, until he made me laugh. In the end he was happy when I settled him in the middle of the turntable, where he could spin properly and not mess around. He cocked his little head and swam past my face at regular intervals with a sardonic smile.

But I forgot to turn off the speaker in Eva's room. The bumps against the pickup arm, the rustles and crackles woke her up.

"For heaven's sake, what are you doing in here?" her voice sounded behind me from out of nowhere.

"I'm taking Rupreeht for a ride on the phonograph," I said.

"What are you doing!" she yelled.

I wondered if I could get away with maintaining that he wanted to. He was going round and round. Eva pushed the switch and the merry-go-round stopped. She glared at me, she was furious, she said,

"What are you turning into? A beast?"

She left.

"A guinea pig!" I replied.

I was leaning my hand on the record player. I had to laugh. The stony animal suddenly gave a twitch, jumped on my hand, buried its little claws in my sleeve and, with an admirable feverishness, it shinnied up my arm. It settled on my shoulder where it gave a clear and audible sigh of relief. I raised my shoulder and bent my cheek to it. It snuggled its head up to me, and at the same time it gave me a firm push. I took it back to its home.

Progress after all, then! But I didn't make much progress with my own homework.

110

XIII

It's so nice out these days that I often walk home from work. I like window shopping, I like looking down from the bridge at the river, I like the girls—bigger ones than you are, dears. Spring is here, you can hear it everywhere, the bands are playing, the birds are singing. In the park, the forsythia is blooming, the grass is greening.

I always pick some of the grass for the guinea pigs. At home, I rinse it with water to get rid of the soot. The guinea pigs squeal and strum the wire mesh on their cage with their little claws, jumping up on it and down again, calling to me that they want their grass already the moment I set foot in the front hall. Pavel, all of a sudden very attentive to their needs, sometimes comes running so he can give it to them; but do you think he ever remembers to bring them some when he is out lollygagging around? No, not him. And so I always tell him, "You're the smart one, aren't you, smarty-pants?" I toss the stook of grass into the hutch, lie down on the floor and rejoice in the sight of the little creatures' wriggling ears and their healthy, undulating fur. I think we feed them well and wholesomely. In the morning they get

oatmeal or grain—we might say that Pavel takes care of pouring
that out for them. In the afternoon, they get some vegetables—
they eat more of those than I do, with the exception of potatoes
—and in the evening we serve them hay, when it is available;
they also used to eat the wood shavings that we put on the floor
of the cage, and when nobody felt like planing wood shavings
for them, they fed on the cardboard laid out in the cage. Now
they have their grass. The first time they got it was when we
realized what grass is and what a guinea pig is, and how they
belong together. They pounced on it like a weasel on a guinea
pig, and nibbled away so hard they bounced. I realized that.
from one point of view, they are essentially beasts of prey. The
turds—that were grey from paper and yellow from wood shavings—turned black, like a goat's, overnight.

Ever since they've been getting green fodder, their residence
has to be cleaned more often, and so Pavel and I have frequent
exchanges.

"And when do you intend to clean the guinea pigs' hutch,
might I ask?" I begin.

"I intended to do it today," he replies circumspectly.

"Why did you abandon your intention?"

"I haven't abandoned it yet. At all."

"Fine, fine," I say. "Except that it would be an interesting
point for both of us, whether you would have done it if I hadn't
reminded you of it just now."

"I probably would have. Not probably, but for sure."

"Except that it'll be supper-time in a little while," I say, "and
so it seemed to me that, what with the stack of reading that has
suddenly accumulated, you weren't going to get around to it any
more today."

"Why shouldn't I get around to it, when I don't happen to
have any accumulated reading?"

"It's a pity that I didn't keep my mouth shut, and that I
didn't write myself a note on a scrap of paper to show you at
bedtime."

"You should have, and then you'd've seen that the hutch
would've been clean."

112

"That's what you say now, smarty-pants!" I yell at him. "But you haven't got any cardboard. I looked in the pantry and there aren't any boxes left. What would you line the hutch with?"

"You mean there's no more cardboard? I didn't know that."

"So that the whole of your speech about how you were going to clean the hutch out for sure, is all of that wiped out, because there isn't any cardboard? Damn it?"

"Well, I'd get me some, if I wanted to clean it . . ."

"If! now it's if! I've got you! A minute ago you said 'for sure'."

"So I will, for sure. And I'll get me some cardboard."

"Where? Where? The stores will be closed in a minute!"

"Well, I'll get hold of some, somehow . . ."

"Somehow, somehow! Nothing was ever done somehow. Anything that was ever achieved in this world was always done in a perfectly precise and particular manner. And not somehow, somehow!"

At that point Pavel finally shut his mouth, and Vašek opened his: "But Dad, any particular manner in which anything was ever achieved could only have been described as 'somehow' to start out with."

I turned to him: "You? I don't recall having asked you anything. But very well, Vašek. Excellent. From now on you'll be the one I'll ask whether Pavel cleaned the hutch."

"Very well, and I'll give you a truthful answer."

"And what will your answer be, for the most?" I asked.

"For the most part, that he hasn't cleaned it."

"Well, then, I'm sick and tired of both of you and you get on my nerves and I'm going to throw the guinea pigs out of the window. Nobody is asking you to tell me that the hutch isn't cleaned; from now on it'll be up to you to see that it is cleaned. From now on!"

I finished and shut the door behind me. I still heard Vašek saying, "Very well."

And now, my dear young reader, would you be interested in finding out whether the guinea pigs' home was cleaned that day? I'll give you one guess!—You're wrong, it was. When Eva heard

113

what the shouting was about, she went in the closet and threw all the Sunday shoes out of their boxes and placed the cardboard right in Pavel's hot little hand.

"Why did you do that?" I asked her. "Just to make me mad?"

"No," she said, feigning innocence. "On the contrary: Just so you wouldn't have to get mad."

"Don't you know what I'm trying to do?" I asked her.

"Of course I know. To harass Pavel."

"To teach him to take care of something on his own! Smarty!"

"Well, then, I did what I could to help, didn't I?"

Nuts, what's the use!

I like to lie on the floor and observe the placid life of the guinea pigs. It's as if the front wall of a house got peeled away; I watch the inhabitants go through motions, take steps and do their little jobs, confident that no one is watching them and that no one has the right to prevent them from doing anything. When he is on my table, Ruprecht always raises his paw to his ear as if he had stolen it, or as if the ear had just been lent to him and could be re-appropriated at any moment, so he hesitates to call attention to it. In his residence, however, he scratches away to his complete satisfaction. Albínka, on her part, washes her dainty face, licks her fur, even her behind, and anybody who wants to comment on that will show himself as a dirty mind. Ruprecht begins to coo, and approaches her with an undulating shuffle, while she starts to object in advance when he's still a foot away, and goes and takes a bite of carrot. They saunter from corner to corner, arguing over blades of grass, poking their little snouts in the wood shavings. And I too, I can go to any corner I want, I can sit at the table or lie down on the couch or on the floor; I get up, I take a picture off the wall, examine it and hang it up again, and there is nothing anybody can do to me. The only thing anybody can kiss, when I select a book of delicate poetry from the bookcase, is my ass. I can read any damn page I please, I can take and sweep a whole shelf of books onto the floor, and kick them to pieces, if Eva isn't home; and if she should walk in and say so much as a word, I would sweep another shelf on the floor, or, if it should suit my fancy, I could grab my hat and run out on the street, where there isn't much I can do any more. Was this enlightened thought what my colleague Karásek had in mind when he brought up the significance of guinea pigs?

They walk around each other, the guinea pigs, and—for reasons that I will never be able to fathom—they chirp at each other like excited robins, or else they cluck like hens. They chew their claws. They tear pieces of paper. And watching them, I pick my nose and aimlessly allow my thoughts to touch on a variety of topics as they flit in and out of my mind: on Pavel and on young ones, then on Vašek and the sewer, then on the bank, and barrels, then guinea pigs again; on carrots and on soup, on Maelstrom and on the canteen, on the canteen and on money, on Eva and the blue jacket, on the sewer and on the bank, on the bank and on barrels in the bank, and so forth. And round again, on the bank and on the band, on money and on Eva, on Eva and on the weasel, on the weasel and the red piglet on the fiddle, on fiddles and basses, on money in a canteen, on Eva in school, on Vašek in the sewer, on the sewer and the sewage, on the sewage in the bank and on and on. And round again on Vašek in the sewer, on the bank and the canteen, and the canted canteen, the soup in the canteen, on stirring the soup, on the band, the bank, the cant, the canteen, the stir, on the band in the bank, on the piglet in the fiddle, on me in the stir, on Maelstrom in the barrel, and on and on and on. So I ponder and I pick, and what I come up with, I toss in the cage with the guinea pigs, where it gets lost in the hay. And on the crazy little girl, too.

When I pick too much grass, we don't give it all to the guinea pigs at once, because it might start to go bad under foot and make them sick. After we wash the soot off, we spread it out on some newspapers in the bathroom until it dries out.

I reached inside the cage, and there was some scrabbling around in there until the smaller of the guinea pigs landed in my hand—it was Albínka, the female. I placed her on my left forearm. She snuggled up to me, her legs straddling my arm to keep her balance. Her head was small and narrow, slender. But with her legs apart, she was actually sitting on her tummy, and it flattened to either side, bloated. She's probably going to have babies. I weighed her in my hand and it seemed to me that there must be a bunch of tiny embryos inside her; she looks out for them when she looks out for herself; when she fears for herself, it is them she is fearing for. To her, her young aren't anything but her innards and her lungs—for that matter, you can't live without lungs, can you? I stood her on the floor in front of the cage. She blinked right, and left, and whoops! she just plunked a claw on the wire mesh and she was home. Ruprecht gave a cluck.

I reached inside the cage, and there was some scrabbling around in there until the larger of the guinea pigs landed in my hand—the dextrorotatarian Ruprecht, that dear fool and unfortunate one. I took him to the bathroom; it was late at night again, and I put him in the tub without any water in it, because guinea pigs don't swim. They don't swim—I pass this information on to you as it was passed on to me. Ruprecht keened his eyes and ears as he found himself on the cool inimical surface; in a damned odd white environment, rising in a curve all around him. Did he wait fifteen minutes? Oh, no, in fifteen seconds he started out with a creeping two-step to investigate his position. What he saw of it did not please him one bit. But he observed that his position rose smoothly upward in all directions, and so he squatted down in the middle of his position and sat there. He looked around in twitches, looking everywhere at once, but I'm not really sure of that. I have yet to find out whether a guinea pig's protuberant popeyes see an entire hemisphere of its universe equally sharply and clearly, when the beams of its totally separated eyes could intersect only with a great deal of difficulty. A guinea pig's eyes are not very mobile. A guinea pig doesn't roll its eyes, it doesn't lift its gaze, it doesn't squint and it doesn't blink. It only winks now and then, under normal conditions about once every ten minutes, and when it does, each eye winks separately.

A guinea pig, its name was Ruprecht, and I knew it well, was sitting in the bathtub with its chin slightly raised, its eyes popping more than ever, totally lacking in opinion or plan. Motionless. Waiting, tensed by everything and for everything that might come to it. Like maybe only a light tap on the tub, the squeak of a sole on a floor tile, my own heavy and audible swallowing made it jerk its ears and twitch its nostrils. It was silent. Does it know me? It ought to. But it didn't get up and walk over to its acquaintance, to call up from its depths and say, "Hey, old Vašek, is it you? Don't you know how I got into this cruddy hole?"

But it doesn't say a word; okay, I'd be satisfied if it recognized me without speaking, naturally, or spoke in its own language, or at least with a gesture, by an effort of will and fervent desire. Can you see me at all, little beastie? And you don't know me? You're afraid of me? You don't trust me? You don't trust anybody? Do you remember your home at all, your wood shavings, your carrots and your mate, and do you want to have it all back, ever? You know what could happen now? You won't even try to jump the foot and a half it would take? Where did you ever get the idea that one doesn't squeal at the base of a cliff, that one doesn't cry out in an enamel pit? Why don't you pull all your strength together, while you have it, because there's still time, and try all the wildest efforts of self-rescuing that might gain divine approbation, if only by their insane hopelessness?

I turned the right-hand faucet. Cold water splashed down and flushed out again into the sewer through the dark opening on the bottom. The guinea pig backed off and raised its gaze even more intensely to the edge of the tub. It gave a nervous wink of its eye, or rather half its face twitched. Its nose got longer. It turned in place in rapid little leaps. Drops of the water splashing hard off the bottom spattered it. But it seemed more frightened by the sound of the catastrophe than by its content. Although the water was flowing out of the tub, a little of it did collect in the bottom. The shallow puddle soon reached the guinea pig's feet. It backed off some more, climbing a little way up the gentler slope at the head of the tub, but it slid back down, of course. It turned in the opposite direction and ran into the water. It ran around all the walls, shaking the water off its feet. It stopped and tried to lick it off. It got its snout wet, sat on its little butt with the intention of wiping it with its front feet, but that just made it get even wetter. It gave up, it threw in the towel, it lost its will and its courage, it had exhausted all its ideas, it called it quits, it was weak and floppy, it didn't give a damn, all it did was to bristle the fur on its

117

nose, drop open its mouth, it began to tremble, its teeth chattered. Quickly, so it wouldn't suffer from the cold, I turned the left-hand faucet and let the warm water flow. The water began to collect even faster. The guinea pig still didn't stir, but I think it must have been grateful for the rise in the temperature of the water. As the water rose, the guinea pig rose too, although it ordinarily doesn't stand around on its hind legs, but rather squats like a hare or a rabbit. Now it stood on its hind legs, though, and raised its body above the water level. It could still touch bottom. It started off on one last exploration—this time on tiptoe—of its position, which I must admit was pretty rotten, and it stopped near me, by me, in front of me and with me. "Well, how are things?" I said gently. "Not so hot," it replied, and rocked slightly in the waves. But it was still standing on its feet. It raised its head, up, in my direction.

I turned off the water. The silence was a relief. Only the sewer gurgled. I became aware of a pressure in my skull, a drunken excitement that I had never known before, a tremor of the nerves. I reached into the pit. With my miraculous power, I lifted Ruprecht into the air, he grabbed my hand with all his claws, he hung on. I picked him up to my cheek and I could hear his tight, thin, wheezing breathing. I also whispered to myself, "We're saved."

XIV

But nothing is as tragic as it seems at the outset: a guinea pig actually swims quite well, as was experimentally determined at a later date. And as for me, I didn't let myself be permanently put off, and one pretty Saturday afternoon, I set out to investigate the house under the viaduct in Hlubočepy.

Nature had already veiled its dirty complexion with a light green habit, which is fine as long as you don't slip and roll down the hillside in a light summer suit. But I wore clothes that were fairly old, and dark. First, I played on the hillside with the boys until a little before evening, when I led Vašek and Pavel into the valley, aimed them toward the trolley car, and told them to give my regards to Mom. They were very surprised, they kept refusing to proceed to the trolley car, they kept coming back and I had to throw rocks at them for a while until they took off.

I climbed up the slope to the railroad tracks, crossed them, and advanced along the hedge to the garden up behind Mr. Maelstrom's house. The garden was a small one; it had two pear trees gone wild, and three decaying plum trees that were still holding their own; the ground at their foot was sprinkled with white

119

petals. The garden came to an end above the house, dropping off suddenly into a cliff, with the edges and faces of crumbling boulders sticking out of it; the yard was actually dug out of the hillside. It was a typical old cottage with an unused pump; the grass grew out of the cracks between cobblestones, and a path was trodden between the door to the cottage and the brick outhouse at the base of the cliff. Stairs leading to the garden were hewn out of the cliffside, but they were almost buried under soil and debris, and beside the steps stood a brick shed, low and narrow, probably a woodshed, and they might have had a sty in there at one time or another.

I settled down under a tree in the corner of the garden, concealed by the lowermost branches, and gazed at the house and the yard. I didn't know what I was waiting for and whether anything interesting was supposed to happen. Without half trying, I had discovered where Mr. M. lived, just when I had begun to devote much of my thinking time to him. Unless of course I was mistaken, and it wasn't the old gentleman at all. I could think of nothing more ingenious than to sit under a plum tree and over his little house, staring down into his yard. I found myself wondering once again at the fact that a man like him, who had been a fairly well-placed bank official during the First Republic, should live like a common laborer or trolley car conductor. Could it be that his wife—if it was truly he—keeps chickens and rabbits? Or maybe even a goat? I don't know a thing about the fellow. Does he still have a wife, or does he live here with a daughter that married a trolley-car conductor? Or does he live alone here, oddly satisfied? The only thing I understood at this point was the canteen. Its contents could easily be meant for a pig's trough. And why oddly? Naturally!

It was a one-storey house, it looked as if it might contain four rooms or so. The entrance was in the back, through this yard here, across a little wooden porch which was badly in need of a coat of paint. Mr. M. was apparently not for those people who substitute several coats of enamel for necessary repair, maintenance and investments. True, he must live alone here. If there were a younger person living with him, the little house would long since have been remodelled, be-toileted, and topped by a television antenna, which apparently isn't apparent. And his old lady, if there were one, would have at least started a plot of parsley, and a daughter would have planted flowers along the cement walk leading from the front gate around the corner of the house to the porch. So I just sat there and waited: probably for the old man to come shufflling out into the yard in his felt slippers. And that would be it, and I would be able to go about my business.

The boys ought to be home by now. They'll be telling their mother that father sends his regards and that he isn't coming. Eva will express her surprise and she will finish her Saturday cooking in deep thought. If she were to take a look in my drawer and notice that I had taken my flashlight and my hunting knife, a veritable dagger, she would be frightened.

"And what did he tell you?"

"Nothing. To go straight home."

"And when will he be home?"

"He didn't say."

"And where was he going or what had he with him or when will he be home—what did he say at all?"

"He didn't say anything, he really didn't."

"So you shouldn't have left. What a dope!"

I could hear the puffing of a train in the distance. It pleased me to realize that I would have a good view from here. We wait for it for half a day, and now that they're gone, the train comes. My chronometer said exactly half past, but it didn't say half past what, because the little hand had broken off when I was rolling down the hillside. It was tumbling around under the crystal, which was also cracked but still in its place. In the yard, nothing moved. I noted with satisfaction that the air directly over the chimney was quavering. I wasn't disappointed; the train slid beautiful and visible out of the turn; it was a freight, and it crept over the viaduct until the entire structure rumbled. Heavy smoke swirled over the valley. There were eighteen cars; the last one was carrying a load of fresh lumber, and there was another locomotive bringing up the rear. It turned out later that this hind locomotive was being driven by thieves. When I looked back to the house, I started. Mr. M. was standing in the yard, welcoming a visitor. And that visitor—I couldn't be mistaken at a distance of a scarce thirty yards—was the well-known bank clerk, my colleague Mr. K. Well, what do you know!

The old gentlemen was not being particularly formal in his greeting of his guest; they didn't even shake hands, or else I had missed that part of it. The old gentleman had on a pair of baggy pants, and a grey sweater that buttoned down the front over his shirt, which was open at the collar. That might mean that Mr. K. had arrived unexpected, which was hard to imagine, but on the other hand, it didn't seem probable that Mr. M. would greet a guest whom he had been expecting in such a casual state of dress. Another explanation occurred to me, as evidenced by the informality with which they greeted each other: Mr. K. is a frequent visitor at Mr. M.'s. The old man must have just come out to unlock the gate while I was meticulously counting freight cars.

The visitor was wearing a pale brown raincoat; there was a hat on his head, and in his left hand he carried a parcel. He wiped his feet and started up the porch steps behind the old man, who was telling him something, turning to him and making slow bony gestures. One of the gestures was aimed at me; they even looked right at me, but I didn't panic; I recognized the illusion. Of course, whatever they were talking about and looking toward must have been in the woodshed directly under me: the two men walked over, the younger one leading the way with a light and firm gait, the older one behind, his joints cracking. The old man was moving his lower jaw. They disappeared behind the woodshed. I noticed that they had left that thing, that parcel, on the steps to the porch. Then the two men returned to the cottage, the visitor picked up the present he had brought, but the old man told him something and made a motion with his hand that might accompany the words, "You can leave that out here." The visitor put the parcel down on the step. That meant that it wasn't a present, or else that it wasn't a surprise for the old man, but in either case it was something that by nature belonged outside. The two men entered the cottage and I could sit here for an hour or more, and that thing would just be sitting on the steps.

A cloud of smoke flew up from the chimney; Mr. M. had poked the fire and added some fuel; the visitor had sat down at the table. If you are struck by the immediate urge to do something risky, dangerous or naughty, you either give up the idea, or else you do it at once. Cruel hesitation just deprives you of the self-assurance that you are the master of your actions. I crept out of my hiding place, ran across the garden, and slid down rather than descended the hidden stairs to the yard. For six months I had been mulling, figuring, poring over maps, contemplating and stewing, guessing and questioning matters that I can't discuss with a living soul if I don't want to get punched, I end up initiating a reconnaissance mission, only to neglect to examine something that can't have anything to do with the whole affair? Not to examine what kind of a present my colleague K. brought to the old gentleman M.?

It was a cardboard carton, tied round with some kind of string, with several openings punched in the top. Lifting it up in my hand was only to give myself some idea of how many of them were in there. I picked the box up, and the bottom began to collapse with warmth and moisture. I tipped back a corner of the lid. There were about six of them, multicolored, white and rusty, about three months old. They wiggled their heads in excitement and kept emitting irritated squeaks. It was a thrilling sight for me. One of the rusty ones was the first to get up; he jumped on the backs of his brothers, and began to scratch his way out of the box, apparently intending to walk back to Prague. I stuck it back and bent the lid back to its original position.

I turned to have a look at the shed at the base of the cliff. I expected to see a rabbit hutch, with or without the rabbits, a goat pen without a goat, an old deserted chicken coop. The rear wall, built up against the cliff, was fine. So were the two side walls, on the left and on the right. The roof had survived as well. But the wooden structures of rabbit hutches, the cages and compartments, were gone. Destroyed, removed, long since burned in the kitchen stove. The shed contained a pile of coal in one corner, a stump for splitting kindling, a few logs and several old pieces of two by four. In the other corner, standing on brick pillars, was a cage. The cage appeared to me—I was approaching it—to be nailed all round with sheet metal. The door—I was standing right by it—was covered with a dense metal screen. And inside—I could see now—it wasn't a rabbit hutch, inside, behind the secure screen mesh, like a little demon, a weasel was pacing. It was a murderer's cage!

I was still staring, tremulous with amazement, at what I had discovered when I heard a light puffing. I raised my eyes to the railroad track. What I saw there was something similar: at a slow carriage velocity, smokelessly and effortlessly, that locomotive was returning; it made some prudent noises atop the viaduct and then it disappeared—along with that one last car, loaded with lumber. The engineer and the fireman were concealed behind the green wainscoting of the machine, crouching down to the floor so no one would recognize them.

I was still staring in amazement after what I had seen when the door to the house gave a creak and voices were audible from the porch. I knew that I wasn't adroit enough to make it back up to the garden in time. Should I run toward the house, fly past it and make for the highway? The gate was closed, perhaps locked. I jumped twice in place out of sheer desperation. The outhouse! I rushed toward it when I noticed that there was another door next to the woodshed, a door leading directly into the cliffside. I ripped out the peg that was stuck into the latch, slipped inside and pulled the door shut behind me. The peg was left hanging by its string; I obviously wasn't able to stick it back in the latch. It was a cellar built into the rock, the way they often do it in the country. It seemed that I had made it in time; the voices outside were talking about something that had nothing to do with me. The old gentleman said, "How many are there?"

"Seven," replied the visitor.

"They're nice," mumbled the old man.

I froze at the visitor's next words: "Aren't you going to give her something now? I'd like to see it."

"Why not? Come on."

I not only heard the shuffling footsteps, I felt them on my hide. They stopped about two yards away from me. I heard a familiar clucking. Then the sound of metal on metal. No one spoke. I pictured the jerky movements of the little head, the frightened eyes, the nervous quivering of the tiny nose. The feet spreading reflexively in the air, and then every which way on the floor. A frightened shriek, a hoarse mewling, then for three seconds nothing and finally a long, interrupted, gently throaty calling, fading and weakening, "*ooeeee ooeeee . . .*" the like of which I had never heard before. The weakness that I felt in my knees, the coldness in my spine, the wave of faintness that flushed through me, all that shows you whom I was feeling for. But what about the sweetish taste in my mouth, the rapid pulse in my throat, the splitting tension in my skull and the spasms of my nerves, for whom was that? And above it all I still heard a voice that sliced into my ears, that calm statement, "I'd like to see it."

Then the visitor said, "Mmmyeah."

And then, I was aghast to hear the old man shuffle over to my hiding place and, with what must have been a simple motion of his hand, insert the peg that was hanging there into the latch. The two men then walked over to the gate. I heard their farewells; the shuffling footfalls crossed the cement and ended inside the cottage.

I leaned against the door; it was useless, but I leaned hard anyway. I could tell through the cracks that the day was coming to a close, but my entertainment had only just begun. I shone my flashlight on my wristwatch. It was precisely a quarter past. The crystal was gone by now too, that meant that the hand had fallen out. It was useless to try and find it, but I did dig around a little in the soil at my feet, and I found the two halves of the crystal. I picked them up and put them in my pocket, the way you are supposed to. Then I looked around in the light of my flashlight.

The cellar was high enough but surprisingly shallow. The back wall was covered by some shelving, which was so full of junk that I had to take a better look at it. And I was right; after I had cleared out the middle section, and moved a board to one side, I discovered another door. It was locked with a heavy padlock. I replaced everything back on the shelves. It wasn't a way out, but on the other hand, it was food for thought. Up until that moment I had considered, if worst came to worst, banging on the door when the old gentleman came out in the yard. Now it didn't seem like such a good idea any more.

I got to thinking that a pretty funny and shamefully banal thing had happened to me, when all of a sudden a shiver of terror ran down my spine. Without warning and without any preliminary sound, the door right in front of my face opened, and there stood—Vašek, my son.

"All right, poor little daddy of ours, you can come out now," he said softly.

But for a moment my fright precluded any motion. When I pulled myself together, I said, "For God's sake, what took you so long?"

He didn't answer me until we got up to the garden where Pavel was waiting for us under a tree.

"The gentleman who left a while ago, well he didn't really leave," Vašek explained. "He crossed under the viaduct and climbed up the other side of the embankment to the tracks, and sat right here and watched the house. He didn't leave, finally, until just a minute ago, the odd gentleman."

We crossed the tracks and descended to the creek. We proceeded toward town along the path by the creek rather than along the road.

"Everything indicates that you disobeyed me, gentlemen."

"No," said Vašek.

"And why."

"Your throwing rocks at us made us wonder," Pavel said in a whisper.

"You can talk out loud now," Vašek reminded him.

"Your throwing rocks . . . " Pavel resumed, this time out loud.

"You said that," Vašek noted.

"But why didn't you go home when I ordered you to?"

"If you want to know something more important, Dad,"

126

replied Vašek, "then I think that the old gentleman, you know, he knew you were shut in there."

"He wouldn't have had to," said Pavel.

"But he could have," said Vašek.

While they were arguing and I wasn't listening, we arrived at a tavern. We went inside and I ordered the boys a Kofola and a beer for myself.

"You know I broke my wristwatch?" I said.

"Then we have suffered a loss," declared Vašek gravely.

"Somewhat diminished by our gains," said Pavel equally gravely as he took a small rusty guinea pig out of his pocket.

I looked at the guinea pig. The boys were laughing. The little guinea pig looked around intelligently and then ran across the table.

"Everything to its purpose," I said, finally.

"And you know how I got it."

"How could I know?"

"When you went to look at that rabbit hutch, I suddenly saw this sweet, pretty little rusty guinea piglet climbing out of the box that was standing there, and it hid under a bucket. So I went and found it, later on."

"When?" I wanted to know.

"When they left."

"You mean you went to find the guinea pig and nòt me?"

"He was rescuing the guinea pig," said Vašek, "and I was rescuing you."

"I would have gotten out of there myself, you know," I said.

"Certainly," said Vašek.

"How many guinea pigs did the old man have in the rabbit hutch?" asked Pavel.

"That wasn't a rabbit hutch," I said.

"Well, in the cage then."

"There weren't any guinea pigs in there," I said.

"What was in there, then?"

"Nothing. It was empty."

We rode home. At home, the boys told Eva all that had happened. I didn't try to stop them. I didn't tell anything. I was

127

very tired. And I don't know what to do with all those guinea pigs, with Albínka expecting young ones on top of it.

I went to bed early, without doing any arithmetic.

I'd like to see it.

XV

The new guinea pig is little, but it's lively. It is rusty-brown, with a few white spots. The boys started calling it Red the Second, which I don't really care for, since it isn't a descendant of the first. But people frequently let themselves get carried away by the urge to give something a telling name, unaware of the fact that it doesn't really tell a thing. The new little Red introduced himself into the household of our dear little pair with a surprising matter-of-factness, without deliberation, without consideration—one might even say shamelessly, as far as Albínka was concerned, with no regard for Ruprecht. Red the Second is a male, small but bright and chipper. His delicate chirping and a few tactful approaches to the white beauty were all the efforts that he was permitted to exert. It isn't so much a matter of the fact that Ruprecht is there to snap at him, the youth showed no fear of that; the main thing is the remoteness of the female, who is on the verge of parturition. She will not allow anything to disturb her meditation or her feeding, she won't even give him a second glance, she just shoves him away with her belly whenever he shows the desire to tangle whiskers with her, and when he approaches her from behind, she kicks him with a foot. He flies away, losing not a hint of his good mood, as he is very light in comparison to her. Then he goes off someplace to read or play or just sit around and watch. I have a feeling that I am finally seeing a normal, untraumatized animal. That is why I don't subject it to any trials or tests, in order that I do not displace it morally or mentally. You, little buddy, escaped the weasel with your life, and you deserve to keep it. It will be whatever you make of it.

The new guinea pig lets nothing disturb him; he pushes his way to feed between his bigger colleagues, and when they chase him off, he digs into the carrot a little way off. This leads me to believe that he comes from a large family. My colleague K. must have a lot of guinea pigs! The rusty guinea pig, accustomed to a collective, knows how to behave in keeping with his age and rank, with the clear prescience that later on, everything will improve for the better, when his little teeth and genitals grow a little larger.

"That is strange," noted Pavel. "The little one isn't afraid of the big one at all, even though he could never beat him up. But maybe," he continued, "maybe that's because the big one doesn't really go after him any. He just chases him away from his food and from his female, and then he quits paying attention to him."

"Yeah," I said.

"What do you think, Dad," Pavel asked, "when Red the Second grows up a little, do you think he's going to try to fight Ruprecht and get Albínka all for himself, or will he be satisfied to share her with him?"

"Yeah," I said.

"But yeah what?"

"Yeah."

And since I never say "yeah", because I don't like it, Pavel saw that I didn't care to have my thoughts interrupted.

My thoughts, when they do not concern guinea pigs or the bank nowadays, are often on the subject of Eva's crazy little pupil. Somebody's going to up and die on you, teacher, that's what the little Pythia told her sometime back. She was right.

Eva's crazy little pupil died on her. You might think that everything is peace and quiet now, but it isn't. Eva doesn't have any
peace, and she doesn't give me any either.

"She was sick!' As time goes by, Eva is getting more and
more upset.

"Were you unjust to her or anything?" I ask.

"I wasn't, or else I don't know that I was. But I treated her
like a healthy child. That in itself is unjust."

"Unjust on whose part?"

Dear little girls, those of you who have yet to die! What can
I say to you? I clasp my hands—be forgiving, I beg you, that is
the way it has to be.

Otherwise, everything is the same at the bank. Those gentlemen can't surprise me at all any more; I don't even know who
they are. I think that there must be a number of them. Two of
them couldn't possibly carry out the idea that I am thinking of.
I once said—or I may even have written it down here—that
anyone who thinks hard about something can come up with the
same ideas as anyone else. I'm not so stupid as to doubt—even
though I work in the State Bank—that one and one are two.
When I was playing on the hillside with my boys, I fell down
and broke my wristwatch. I lost a hand off the face of it in M.'s
cellar at the foot of the cliff. Imagine the care with which someone must have searched there for K. to place it on my work table
two days later, with the words, "He who seeks, finds, isn't that
the truth, friend?"

"It is, if he knows what he is seeking," I replied.

After this little exchange, it is out of the question for me to
return to the cellar ever again. More's the pity.

Eva is also putting pressure on me, never to investigate at the
old gentleman's cottage, and never to throw rocks at our boys,
and they in turn have received orders from their mother never
to leave me alone. So if I ever want to go to the cottage, I'll have
to go straight from work. And that's why Eva comes to meet me
after work at the State Bank building whenever she can, so I'd
go straight home. Unpleasant, indeed unpleasant. What if I want
to go have a beer, which I don't usually? I'd go have one too,

131

says Eva. And what if I wanted to go see a woman? I'd walk you there and wait outside, she says. Having arranged all that, I still don't know how I'm going to get to the old gentleman's cottage.

Oh, God, I feel sleepy again, terribly, and so I don't know if I'll finish collecting my thoughts, which need collecting, badly. The old gentleman, from whom I would like to buy the cottage, declared a grave danger ensuing from banknotes that our guards are transferring into so-called mysterious circulation, because these banknotes that nobody can locate could be thrown back into circulation later, bringing about a terrible fluctuation in the economy. And this presents an opportunity for a band of saviors simply to replace the disappearing banknotes . . . I know, a number of questions arise, including the problem of where I am to get the money to buy the cottage when I don't have any. But that's something else entirely; the main thing would be for the owner to be willing to sell. But why should he sell if he now has all the banknotes he wants? And besides, the band wouldn't permit the sale of a cottage with a cellar like that. And on top of it all—I am in danger, just for knowing about it, if in fact I know anything at all.

I realize that by talking in riddles this way I am making it even harder for you to understand; but I can't talk any more clearly because I don't want to divulge anything earlier than I want to, and before it is definite and certain that this venture isn't for me, or else that I'm not going to get invited to join it. The fact that they apparently know my every move frightens me, and I wouldn't like them to know about my every thought, meant for the eyes of my young readers. So at night, when I finish my work, I place these papers, along with other notes and computations, into a simple hiding place: under the guinea pigs. I lift the cardboard on the floor of the cage and stick my papers, wrapped in a waterproof envelope, under it. I had to tell Pavel, because he might be surprised when he cleans the cage. When I confided in him, he asked me if I had to.

"I have to," I replied.

"And can I read it?" he asked.

"I'd rather you didn't, son," I answered, if only with an eye to what I had written about his guinea pigs, "because then I wouldn't have anyplace to put anything I don't want anyone to see. So I'd like you to tell me, here and now, whether you intend to read it or not."

"All right, so I don't."

"I'll be happy to grant you some other privilege, in exchange," I said.

"No, I don't want to."

"Why not?" I asked.

"I just don't," he replied. "Because then it wouldn't mean anything, any more."

"What wouldn't?"

"I just want to not read it," he said.

And he doesn't read it, because if he did, I could tell. But sometimes he forgets to stick the papers under the cardboard when he cleans out the cage, and so I have to keep checking up on him.

The guinea pigs, who are on the verge of multiplication, will need a new cage, and I'm going to need to bring home about five thousand crowns from work. When Albínka stands up on her hind legs, resting her front legs on the wire mesh of the cage, her tummy is like a heavy fur droplet. I can feel the young ones in it, and I pointed them out to Eva and both of the boys. Pavel gave a pleased smile, Vašek was more curious than pleased, while Eva is fearful and yet gently moved by the impending event. Outside, it is warm; I'd like to take my family out to observe Nature, but four bicycles are worth about four thousand crowns.

Now all the family is asleep again—just me and the guinea pigs, and I am taking one of them out of the cage. It is Ruprecht, and I am placing him on the table again, examining him and thinking about him. The window is open, and out on the street I can hear the voices of people leaving the tavern downstairs. Although I've lived in this block for many years, if I went downstairs and walked into that tavern, nobody there would know me. I am unknown—no one would know me, would owe me, give credit where credit is due, my credit is due, do you . . .

And I see that I've fallen asleep again. I certainly feel like sleeping. In the meantime, Ruprecht hasn't gotten enough gumption to do anything worth mentioning on the table, except pee all over the state budget again. Ruprecht, Ruprecht! Don't provoke me! You've got a litter of little ones started, and there is nothing to stop you from dying now. Your life would be easy to destroy, your front legs would never resume their innocent stance. When the cloud gathers over our heads, your throat will tighten, your eyes will pop, your nose will cruddle, your heart will huddle. You won't even say Jack Robinson.

I carried the guinea pig into the bathroom, and stood it on the edge of the tub which I had filled with lukewarm water. There was a buzzing in my brain already! The guinea pig jerked his red-eyed gaze all around, listening to the noises to discover what they portend. I watched him trembling there, and wondered if he was of any value at all. Can anyone force anybody to his death? Wow! I measure the half yard distance that the guinea pig needs to jump to the floor and hide under the tub. It justs waits there passively, it doesn't learn. Unless I am merciful, that will be the end of the guinea pig. But I know myself, and I know that I just want to see it struggle, and that I won't let it lose. One doesn't just throw a guinea pig in the water, but it could fall in all by itself, and what if there were no one around to help it? I'm glad that I'm here in time.

And sure enough, the guinea pig began to weave on the tub's edge, until it fell in the water. I fished it out right away and set it back, curious to see what lesson it had learned from the incident. It was wet, it wanted to shake itself, and it fell in again. I fished it out again right away and set it back on the edge of the tub. Its feet were slippery and they slid in all directions; it moved to repair their position and fell in again. Okay, then swim! I left the bathroom and turned off the light.

I am discovering that I made a mistake at the beginning in my decision to write in the first person singular. I am at the end of the possibilities granted by the first person singular. No author would find it easy to write truthfully, "When its head appeared above the water's surface, I pushed it under again, holding it as long as the bubbles kept rising to the surface, and until its wild twitchings turned into a prolonged stiffening of its body, ending in a sudden weakening and limpening, which indicated that he was done for." So far, any author who has ever done this to anybody has written about it in the third person singular, as if it had been someone else who had done it, using this simple trick to detract the attention of readers and critics from his deeds to his words. I started to write this book in my own person, because I thought that it would be a book about the fact that we've got guinea pigs and how we observe them and how they amuse us. At Christmas time, no one could have guessed where it would all end. What should I do now? All I can do is to switch over to the third person, and when I get the time, someday, I'll rewrite the beginning.

The banker left the bathroom and turned off the light. He sat down at his table and began to work on his computations. But he had difficulty doing his work. It got harder to add simple numbers in an unchanging tempo. For moments he couldn't remember how much four and three was, and when a sum amounted to more than ten, it took him several seconds to do it. Shocked, he realized that he had to collect all his will power to keep reminding himself that he must add the next number when in many cases it would have been much easier to subtract it. Finally he developed a mental embolism, with the pressure behind it increasing rapidly.

He flipped his pencil to one side and shuffled over to the bathroom. He opened the door without turning on the light. He wanted to listen. He heard some gentle splashing and light tapping. Then he switched on the light. The white guinea pig was lying stretched out on the surface, its nose several millimeters above the water, slender and smooth and silent as a little torpedo. When it reached the end of the tub, its tooth tapped the enamel surface and it turned back. Occasionally it attempted to jump up and out, but it didn't have anything solid to push off from and so its effort always ended with it falling back deeper into the water, which immediately flooded its nose and eyes, red and open even under the surface. The banker observed all this, wondering what

135

hope the guinea pig had that it would succeed in its efforts, what it was seeing, what it was hearing and what it was thinking. He observed neither despair nor hopelessness, just effort. But it couldn't alter its destiny by means of any effort that it might exert if no one saw it exerting that effort. He turned off the light and sat down on the edge of the tub in the dark, listening. The guinea pig continued. So now he couldn't see, and when he stopped up his ears, he couldn't hear either. But he knew, all the same. And as long as he knew that the guinea pig was in the water, he couldn't think that it wasn't. And also, he was the only person in the world that knew it. From this fact the banker deduced that if there is a God, He is guilty, even if no one, not even a mouse, in this whole world believes in Him. He heard splashing. He turned on the light. The guinea pig, apparently having lost its reason, was now swimming under water. It had turned slightly sideways, arching its back. Swimming under water it was, as if it were equipped to, as if it had arranged to receive a special dispensation. But no, it had no dispensation, it had just become disoriented and swam a little deeper. Its eyes were still open down there, wide and red. It touched the surface from below, poked through with its nose, emerged and gasped for air, and resumed its track back and forth in the tub. Several turds accompanied it up to the surface. You! thought the banker. And when the guinea pig swam past him, he pushed its head under the water. The guinea pig kicked its feet harder and swam away. When its head surfaced again, the banker pushed it back under, and held it there as long as the bubbles kept rising to the surface, and when its wild twitchings turned into a prolonged stiffening of its body, he quickly fished the beastie out of the water. It was stiff and straight, its eyes wide, with the bluish whites finally appearing around the red circles of its iris. The beastie's chest was expanding spasmodically and its limbs were trembling.

I set Ruprecht on a chair, wrapped him up in a towel, rubbed his fur dry all over, wiped out his ears, his paws, dried the fur on his head, even wiped under his chin, fluffed it up so the air could get to it, warmed and wrapped him up, unwrapped him, waited till he wiped his face off with his paws, and finally carried him off to my room where I left him among the pillows for a good half hour. Only then, when I saw that he was going to be all right, did I carry him home.

When I entered the menagerie, Pavel sat up in bed.

"Aren't you asleep?" I whispered.

"Are you putting away your papers?" he answered.

"Yes. Good night." I said.

"I haven't been reading it," he said wanly and lay down again.

"Good boy," I said.

XVI

Pavel is sick and I don't like the look of him. I don't feel like thinking about it, let's rather talk about the bank.

I haven't seen old Maelstrom for several days. I went to have a look at his door, and the key wasn't in it. Our financial system, which I have left unmentioned on these pages for quite a while, is carrying on in the same old tremulous fashion. All talk of the impending threat of a depression has ceased, because everyone has gotten accustomed to the threat, so that when the depression truly does hit maybe we won't even notice it. Or else, it has begun already. Everyone has also gotten used to the intensified searches. They are more attacks than searches, during which we lose everything that the guards find on us. But this leads to days upon days of peace and quiet, when the guards stand and chew the fat by the exits, not noticing us or else speaking to one or another of us, "See you tomorrow!"

My colleague Karásek doesn't run around our financial institution collecting missing banknotes any more, but simply notes their numbers. Various bankers wander in and out, bringing him numbers too, I think. I know what he needs those numbers for! I made a test: I gave him the serial numbers of fifty one-hundred-crown notes that I intended to carry out of the bank on a certain day. He raised his eyebrows, and said, "Well, what do you know! Don't forget, now, tomorrow you let me know, friend."

"Certainly," I said.

The next day I reported that I had succeeded, and so he crossed the numbers off his list. He didn't need them. Need I say more? Of course, these saviors aren't saving anything. By doing what they are doing, they are still not averting the ever-present possibility that the confiscated and vanished banknotes will suddenly appear back in circulation one fine day, and so they'll be circulating in duplicate. I can't believe that old Mr. Maelstrom, the commercial engineer, could have given his approval to such a scheme.

But let's not talk about the bank, children, let's talk about pets, they're nicer. Our three guinea pigs are very happy together. Albínka and Ruprecht have gotten used to having little Red around, and they don't chase him away any more. I often find all three of them cuddled up together, particularly at night. Albínka dozes, Red is asleep outright, only Ruprecht, that Ruprecht! No sooner does he hear me than he wakes up as if he had never been asleep; and then when he sees me, he prepares himself for vigilance. "Sleep, old man, sleep," I usually say, and go back to my nocturnal calculations.

Sometimes I am possessed by the idea that I am little and a guinea pig is big. I'm so little that I barely reach up to his claw, I'm as big as a grain of wheat. And everything looks entirely different, all of a sudden, even though it is all the same. Fat whiskers lean over my being. When I look up, I don't see the sweet and touching, innocent face of the ever-frightened piglet, but a frighteningly apathetic, dull and motionless snout. Above it, a pair of eyes like immense convex lenses, empty and terrifying, without the shadow of a thought behind them. The body of the beast towers high over me; its urine will shortly be up to my waist. I can't stay in place.

Under such circumstances I lose all inclination to talk about animals and I'll talk about Pavel, instead, after all. One morning

139

he simply didn't get out of bed, and when we asked him what was the matter, he replied in a whining voice that it was nothing and that he was getting right up. He got a thermometer. He had a fever. When asked where it hurt, he said he didn't know and that he would go to school.

"No, you won't," said Eva unhappily, "you're sick."
Pavel burst into tears.

"What are you crying about?" I asked.

"Because you're asking me," he responded.

"He's sick," said Eva uncomfortably.

"So he's sick," I said. "Can't he be sick?"

"Well, yes, he can, but . . ." she didn't finish.

"We'll send for the vet," I said with a smile.

"It's too late for that," said Pavel, and burst out crying even harder.

Eva was frightened. Why is it too late? What does the child mean? I didn't know for certain, but what I thought, I kept to myself.

Eva and Vašek were sitting at breakfast in the kitchen, because in a little while they would have to leave the house. I sat down by Pavel.

"What happened to you, Pavel?"

"Nothing happened to me."

"Don't you want to tell me something?"

"I don't want to tell you anything and I'm not going to tell you anything!" his voice rose in volume and pitch.

Then Eva left for school to arrange to stay home, and in the meantime I stayed home. I gave the guinea pigs some grain. I went down to the park to pick some grass for them. I reached into the cage and pulled out these papers of mine. Pavel turned his back and buried himself in his quilt, head and all.

"Pavel, if you're going to have to stay in bed, maybe you'd like me to read you some of what I've written, wouldn't you like that?" I said, but of course, I didn't intend to read him any of it, I was just testing him.

"No, I wouldn't, you can keep it," he said, his back to me.

"You may be sick, but you can still get swatted," I said mildly. I left the room. He ran after me, opened the door a little and

140

called, "When a person says something isn't to be read, he shouldn't change it!"

"You're right," I said. "To bed! On the double!"

Should I take my papers to work, or should I leave them home? Should I remove some pages? Or should I play my fiddle for Pavel? How would the G-D chord affect him?

"Pavel," I said, entering his room, "wouldn't you like me to play my violin for you?"

"You can if you want to," he said.

"No, Pavel, I don't think I will. You'd just get a headache."

Then Eva came home and so I could go to work.

The doctor didn't come to see the patient until toward evening. What could he do? Prescribe some aspirin, and suggest that we let whatever it is come to a head. So far, the only symptoms were the fever, and some feverish statements. By now Pavel was calm; he wanted to read but it tired him out. Vašek read to him, and then I read to him too for a while, but not out of my papers. We wanted to lend him the guinea pigs for a while, but he got very upset because they might catch whatever he had. The female in particular had to be healthy, now of all times.

I set up Albínka's maternity ward, with Pavel watching me from his bed. I took a small wooden box and fixed wheels to it so it would be mobile. Not so much for the guinea pigs (just between you and me, not for them at all) but for Pavel—so he could reach out of his bed to the floor and move the maternity ward back and forth. But he didn't get to do it much, because that same night we took him to the hospital.

It really shook me up, but I controlled myself in order not to intensify Eva's fears.

"He'll be better off there, now that it's come to that," I said.

"But you know how unhappy he's going to be, he hasn't got anything there," said Eva. "He's never been alone among strangers before."

"But he'll get the treatment he needs, quickly and effectively, and he'll be home before you know it," I said. "What worries me is something else. He won't be here when the little ones are born."

We didn't sleep very well at our house that night. Even the

141

female guinea pig, displaced into the maternity ward, was restless. I kept hearing her rattling around and squeaking every so often. Vašek made noises in his sleep. And then morning came, a nice, sunny morning of a pleasantly warm day in the late spring, a morning for which we would have been thankful if everything had been normal; but it wasn't. Pavel wasn't home. During the night, Albínka had escaped from the maternity ward and had climbed back into the cage. Now she sat there calm and satisfied, with her long noble little head, nibbling the grain that Vašek had poured instead of Pavel. When would she have her young ones? Sixty-three days from Day X, that is to say, we don't know when.

Early in the morning, I went to the post office to phone the hospital. I got the head nurse on the phone, but she told me to speak to the head physician, when he comes. She isn't allowed to give information about the physical condition of the patients.

"I don't want any information about his physical condition," I said. "I just want to know how he is, nurse, please. We brought him there during the night."

"I can't tell you that," she said. "You'll have to wait till the head physician arrives."

"There must be some other doctor there, isn't there? Then he can tell me how our boy is."

"Look, mister, I can't go running around trying to find him for you now, you're going to have to call up after they make the rounds."

"All right, thank you. But nurse, I know you aren't allowed to give out any information, but all I want to know is how he is."

"Look Mister, that's just what I'm not allowed to give out, that's just what only the doctor can tell you."

"You mean you don't know?" I said.

"Whether I know or I don't know, listen, you!" she said; and I could sense that she was removing the receiver from her ear and bringing it closer to hanging it up. I yelled, "Well, is he alive or is he dead!"

There was a sudden silence on the phone. Then she spoke: "Go on, for heaven's sake. Why shouldn't he be alive? Nobody died here since yesterday!"

142

I ran home, where Eva and Vašek were waiting to hear the news. Then I went to the bank, where I called Eva shortly before noon. She had gotten through to the hospital in the meantime, and found out how Pavel was. Pavel's fever had gone down a little, but they hadn't started making any tests yet. It was obvious that they didn't know a thing. A bunch of quacks.

But it calmed me down a little, and I felt as if I had been granted some time that I ought to take advantage of. Making a noisy or obvious investigation as to the whereabouts of Mr. Maelstrom was out of the question. But somehow I had to discover, or deduce theoretically where he could be.

When I find out, I'll go to him, address him and suggest that he sell me his cottage. In other words, sirs, it is his cottage I am interested in, and not the national economy; it is entirely senseless for someone to catch me displaying an interest in the old gentleman again, and treat me as if my interest were in the entire national economy. Moving into the cottage would be healthy for the children, and for me too, and for Eva.

Several times in the past few years, sitting at my table at night with my hands folded in front of me, I realized with frosty amazement that a person can do anything he sets his mind to. It's just a matter of really setting your mind to it, and then you can do anything that you think of and that your physical strength can handle. So I appeared to myself as a generator with unfathomed power, power of which I shall never entirely convince myself.

When I finished my work at the office the first day that Pavel was ill, I left simultaneously with my colleague Karásek. I rode down with him and watched him pass by the guards. Then I rode back up to the seventh floor. With a firm gait, without hesitating and without fear, I walked down the narrow corridor. At that hour, when desks were being closed and bankers were leaving, the cleaning ladies stepped onto the scene, one to a floor, and they opened all the doors, took out the waste baskets and vacuumed the rugs. To the buzz of one of those vacuums, I reached the open door behind which it was buzzing, removed the key—the cleaning lady's pass-key—turned on my heel and rode back down.

The cleaning lady will reach for the key, it won't be there, she'll slap her apron pocket, it won't be there either, she'll take off and start to search where she might have left it. I went on home.

When I got home, Pavel wasn't there, he was in the hospital, had been since yesterday. It was the first time we had been short by a child; it is a strange anxious feeling, having one of yours outside your sphere of influence. We discussed it for a while, Eva and I, and then she went shopping and I picked up a guinea pig, put it in my pocket and paced the floor, thinking about problems. Eva came home and began to fix supper. At that hour, Vašek was in his room, or the menagerie, working on his homework, or at least that was what I thought he was doing. It was exceptionally quiet in there. We sat at dinner in silence. Then dinner was over and Vašek returned to the menagerie.

Eva said, "I wonder about our Pavel."

"I wonder," I said.

"What I wouldn't give," she said, "if he were sitting in there, in our little zoo!"

The door opened and there stood Vašek, with a cat in his arms.

"I don't know how to tell you, and I don't know how it happened," he said, "but this cat turned up in our room."

"And it's black," cried Eva darkly.

"You can't fool me with that!" I exclaimed.

"I don't even want to fool you," said Vašek.

"I'll tell you how it got there," I said.

"You do that. I'd appreciate it."

"You brought it," I said.

"I didn't bring it. I'm sitting there doing my homework, and when I look up, there it is, sitting in the middle of the room, looking at the guinea pigs from a distance."

"So it'll get tossed out, and that's that," I said.

"It's up to you," said Vašek.

"Black," Eva repeated.

"So what, there's nothing wrong with black," I said.

Vašek stood there, petting the cat.

"If it wasn't you that brought it," I said, "how would it have found out that we've got guinea pigs?"

"I didn't bring it," he repeated.

"So how did it know?"

"But I don't know how it got in, either," said Vašek.

"Out!" I said.

"All right," said Vašek, and he took the cat out to the foyer, opened the door to the hall and put the cat out on the floor. It didn't move, it just stood there and stared at the door. Before he closed it, he said, "Go on, pretty kitty! And come again!"

XVII

In the morning, a sleepy-eyed Vašek stuck his head in my door and said, "That cat is here. Again."

I jumped out of bed and ran to the menagerie.

"So we throw it out of the window!"

The black cat was sitting quietly in the middle of the room, its front paws pulled up to its chest and its tail curled around its body. It looked at me and then went back to watching the cage with the guinea pigs from a distance. The tip of its tail was squirming.

"Since when has it been here?" I asked.

"I just woke up," said Vašek.

"Who let it in?" I asked.

"I don't know," he answered.

"But I know!" I said.

"Who did?" he asked.

"You."

"Not me."

"Then who, me?" I asked.

"It came all by itself," he said, shrugging his shoulders in his pyjamas.

"I'm just about fed up with those mysteries of yours," I said.

"What mysteries of mine?" he said.

"You and your blue windbreaker, and now this cat."

"I don't have any blue windbreaker," he said.

"But you do have a black cat!" I pointed at the cat.

"Thanks," he said, bending over to pick up the cat.

"Let the cat be and go wash your face," I said.

The balcony door was open. Could a cat climb up to the third floor, somehow, all by itself? I'll just knock it off the balcony, let it show what it can do. I approached the cat, and it got up and walked over toward me. I picked it up. It was a peaceful and trusting cat, a tomcat. A half-grown kitten. I stroked the little tomcat and looked down at the street from the balcony. Of course, I wasn't going to drop him down there. First of all, I don't know if he isn't Pavel, and in the second place, I wouldn't even throw an ordinary tomcat. There are people walking down there.

I took the little tomcat into the kitchen and Eva gave him some milk before we put him out again. I ran to the post office to find out how Pavel was. The doctor told me that his temperature was still high, and that the tests were coming out negative. I didn't know what he was testing and where, I wasn't in the hospital. Aside from blood and urine, I didn't know what they could be testing, unless it might be a chest X-ray.

"The tests are negative," said the physician.

"Tell me, doctor," I asked, "what about testing for his presence, is that at least positive? I mean, is he there at all?"

He laughed and said that he was.

"I wonder if you could do me a huge favor, doctor. Could you take a look in his room and see if he is really and truly in it?"

He left, and two minutes later, he said, "Don't worry. He's right here, in his bed."

I walked home from the post office. The tomcat was sitting by the empty dish. I asked whether he had left the kitchen while I was gone. Both Eva and Vašek assured me that he hadn't. Excellent, excellent!

When Eva and Vašek had turned to their business, I took the

tomcat into the menagerie. I put Albínka in the maternity ward and covered her up with a drawing board. Then I lay down on the floor. The cat stared at the cage and scrunched down on the floor. Then he took a few slinking steps and jumped inside the cage! I turned over onto my hip so I could fish out a long slingshot elastic that I had in the pocket of my pants. The cat lurked in one corner of the cage, spying on the guinea pigs. They returned his gaze with a simple-minded stare. It was clear that, but for me, they were marked out for death. I felt a shiver of excitement. I'd like to see it.

Ruprecht was looking calmly at the unknown creature. Little Red the Second took his place at Ruprecht's side, equally calm. The cat took a step forward, and lightly, as if in jest, reached out for the white mousie. Surprisingly, he didn't run his claw through the pink eye, and the guinea pig wasn't frightened in the least; on the contrary, it approached the cat, curiously and carefully, leaving its hind legs ludicrously far behind. Ludicrous, that means comical. It came all the way to the cat's nose and, with a friendly cluck, sniffed it. The cat stared, incredulous, to the point of retreating a step. And that was when the guinea pig made a mistake, what a shame! though we mustn't hold that against it. What it ought to have done was to maintain its advantage, squealing and advancing, and to take a bite out of that nose. The cat, though equipped with claws that were far sharper than those of the guinea pig, was, as an individual, young and foolish, and as a species, stupid and superficial, incapable of doing anything but attacking anything that was smaller and anything that showed signs of fleeing. It occurred to me that something small but determined, running at him would totally wipe him out. But the guinea pig quit paying any attention to him and began to move about its home freely and fearlessly. Its irregular gait, its fur and its odor, its red eyes, all that must have irritated and fascinated the cat as something fierce. He flattened his ears, twitched the muscles in his back, waved his tail. He stretched out and reached again for the guinea pig. This time it must have been painful, because Ruprecht gave a squeak. Whap! went the elastic and the cat gave a hiss. The banker, lying on the floor, was gleeful. The cat looked around for a while, unable to figure out what had happened. The guinea pigs began to walk around the cage again, burrowing in the hay. The cat crouched back, skulked over and slashed at the white guinea pig again. Zap! and he got hit in the muzzle, and he didn't know by whom or how. The banker and I laughed softly. That's the way! You'll see! Welcome, friend! We've got guinea pigs!

The cat leapt out of the cage and shot under Pavel's bed to hide among all the junk. His eyes shone in the dark down there, observing me. He was suspicious already. I didn't stir. After a while, the cat crept out, and—at a safe distance from me all the while—aimed for the balcony door. But on the way, his eye fell on the cage and that intrigued him so much that he stopped. Mice! Look at that! thought the cat and a rare opportunity seemed to be presenting itself. Thinking that if he reached them unobserved, he'd have them, he started to creep across the bare floor like an Indian scout hiding among the tree trunks. Although I'd like to see a guinea pig getting throttled, I had no intention of allowing him that pleasure. He was at the cage already, he had jumped up on the mesh, and as he jumped, he revealed his butt to me for a second, and thwap! he'd gotten it there. He flew out as if he had landed on a grenade, circled the room giddily, and fled to the balcony, where he stopped. The banker went out after him. The cat ran back into the room and took up a sorrowful position by the door. The banker opened all the doors for him, all the way to the outside hall. The cat left without so much as a thank you, but the banker was well brought up and remembered his manners, and so called down the stairs after him, "Drop by again tomorrow!"

I left for the State Bank, where I recalled several times that day what had happened to the cat that had wanted to eat up our guinea pigs. I was delighted and couldn't wait till the next day.

But what I wanted to tell you was how the first thing I did when I got to the bank was to go up to Mr. Maelstrom's office. Again, without any divisive reasoning, simply in the certainty that anything I want to do, I'll do it, if I want to badly enough. I unlocked the door with the key I had picked up, and walked in.

As I entered the room, I could smell the dead, motionless air, full of the odor of paper, cigarette smoke and floorwax. I could even discern a trace of a sourish smell, either from soup or from the old gentlemen's shoes. Otherwise nothing had changed; the room had not been put to any other use if the old gentleman is on vacation. Nothing new on the desk, not even a scrap of paper, just an inkwell, a pen, a blotter, the key in the lock of the desk drawer, with a bunch of keys dangling from it, just like it was before. I walked to the wardrobe. As I expected, there was no trace of the canteen, nor, of course, of the grey coat and hat. I looked in the space behind the desk—the barrel was gone!

At that point, I was incapable of coming up with a preliminary auxiliary theory, and I remain incapable of it. Had the old gentleman moved? How can you carry a barrel out of a bank? Had he really moved though? I stepped to the table and grabbed the key . . . he had left all his keys behind. Had he left them? Forgotten them? I opened the drawer. It was empty. Only tufts of dust, some wire paper clips. I opened the drawers one by one, left and right. In one of them I found the bank telephone directory and an old brown manilla file folder. All it had in it, though, was clean paper (and I feel like adding, otherwise they wouldn't have left it). Unruled paper, several sheets, a couple of sheets of paper with lines, and graph paper, the printing pale blue, also in sheets. I picked up the little pile of papers and riffled the edges with my thumb. Some writing flashed past on one of the sheets of paper. A single piece of paper with writing on it, forgotten among the rest. It was written in indelible pencil, and began: "Esteemed Sirs:" The writer must have re-evaluated his attitude toward the recipients, because he had struck out the original greeting and changed it to "Sirs!" Two lines, only two, followed: *In view of the fact that my most expert opinion concerning the conclusion of an international lombard agreement, which is unheard-of, has remained unacknowledged . . .* That's it. The end. I didn't know what the old engineer was actually referring to as being unheard-of—whether it was the international lombard agreement or the lack of an acknowledgement. I turned the sheet over, and on the reverse was something that I consider to be a second version of

150

the original text. The writer had apparently given up on the first version, about the way a sensible person gives up all hope of coming to an understanding with a deadhead, and instead of giving reasons, simply ups and swears. Because the second version reads: *Sirs! Your villainous scheme to place the republic in lombard* . . . Unfinished, and I could find no other version anywhere. Had he completed one and sent it off? And to whom? Apparently it was some lombard or other that the writer considered unheard-of. But what was that lombard, anyway? Who knows? Where can we find out? I picked up the folder, locked the desk, and took the keys, too. Now I have all of it home in the cage.

Eva phoned me after noon. She had been to the hospital, but they wouldn't let her in to see Pavel; they said it was so as not to upset him, now that he had calmed down a little. She began to cry over the phone; there hasn't been any improvement, that means he's worse, because if he doesn't eat and he still has a temperature, he's just getting weaker. And the doctors can't find a thing.

"I'm frightened . . . " she wept.

"Quit annoying me with all those frights of yours!" I raged cheerfully. "Do you think I don't know what it is that you're frightened of again? But try saying it out loud, and you'll see for yourself how impossible it sounds."

"Hurry home, will you?" she pleaded.

I promised I would, but it wasn't easy. I would have liked to ride out to the cottage by the viaduct. Whom should I ask? I'm in it all by myself. The barrel has disappeared from Mr. Maelstrom's office. Six months ago, I was convinced—under the suggestive description of a depression in Poe's study *Descent into the Maelstrom*—that the old commercial engineer was keeping a barrel in his office so he could use it to save his life, because a barrel was the best shape to withstand the sucking force of the whirlpool. And like a real fool, proud of how clever I was, I began to search for the Maelstrom, and I found it, too. And now the barrel is gone, Mr. Chlebeček alias Slobechek is gone. And as for myself, self-educated by my own meditations since that time, I'm now most inclined to believe that Mr. Slobechek must have finally put up some sauerkraut in his barrel, so he'd have something put by for worse times that were to come. Because it is deeds, deeds that are good for anything, as opposed to meditation. And somewhere, somewhere, a horrible lombardment is being planned that will leave us gasping.

At home, I succeeded in calming the frightened Eva down a little, although unfortunately, my own state of mind was worsened in the process. A constant fever and a high sedimentation rate, loss of weight and apathy, all that without any determinable cause, what would become of Pavel?

After supper, Eva and I sat over some tea. I took all of our guinea pigs and put them on the table where we were sitting. They gathered in a cluster and they encouraged each other by cooing, squeaking and touching.

"That old engineer that I told you about," I said, "has come up with a pretty serious matter: they're planning the lombardment of the republic."

"You mean bombardment," said Eva.

"Lombardment, damn it! I know what I'm saying. I just don't know what it is, unfortunately. Unfortunately."

"And you never told me about any old engineer," said Eva.

"And I'm not going to, either. Because all your commentaries make me mad."

"Sorry," she said sadly, and patted my hand.

"Isn't it picturesque?" I indicated the guinea pigs all over the table.

"It's nice," she said, in the same sad tone of voice. "I wonder what Pavel is doing now?"

"Lying there having a fever." I said.

The guinea pigs took off across the table, bravely and collectively.

"Aren't you worried about him?" Eva asked in an irritated tone.

"Look out!" I exclaimed, "can't you be careful?"

Albínka had almost fallen off the table by her.

"You're more concerned about the guinea pigs than about the child," she said.

152

"I can't do anything about the child," I said, "but I can do something about the guinea pigs! It isn't a matter of being concerned right now! You can be careful so that Albínka doesn't fall off the table. Right now, Pavel is mostly concerned about her."

The guinea pigs grew bolder and began to run all over the table. Ruprecht first, behind him Albínka, with Red the Second taking up the rear. Lined up one behind the other that way, they looked like a line of guinea pigs, but also like a train. They rode over the table. Eva was being careful now.

We watched little Red approach Albínka. It was comical, his thin growling, his cuddling his cheek up to her side, wriggling his little butt like a dandy in jodphurs and then flattening it out on the floor. Ruprecht didn't try to chase him off, but just when they ran into each other on a curve, he snapped at him lightly. But Red the Second went on with his dance. They felt perfectly at home on our table. We would have all felt pretty good, if nothing had happened. I thought of Mr. Chlebeček. Putting up sauerkraut? Now, in the spring?

"Don't we have a piece of lettuce?" I asked.

Eva didn't have any lettuce, but she had a turnip cabbage. She took a leaf of it, washed it off and placed it on the table. The guinea pigs gathered around the leaf and pulled it in all directions. When little Red got too close to Ruprecht, he got bitten in the ear.

"Look at him bite!" cried Eva. "Nasty old bull!"

I'd been thinking of asking her for a while already, and so I asked her, "Which one do you like?"

"I like her the best," said Eva.

That upset me. I'd just as soon prevent that. "But she is mostly Pavel's. He got her for Christmas," I objected. "Let's say that each of us had one guinea pig, which one would you pick?"

"I like the little one here."

"I like all of them," I said. "But if I were going to choose a guinea pig, I know which one I'd choose. And you, which one would you choose?"

"This sweet little rusty one," she said.

It still wasn't clear enough. I gave my query more precision: "If you were to say which guinea pig is yours, what would you say?"

153

"That this one is mine," and she pointed directly and indisputably at Red the Second. "Look at that ugly old bull of a Ruprecht, see how mean he is to him? Look at that!"

And she slapped Ruprecht across the back.

"I have a better idea." I said.

Little he-piglet, I thought to myself, it would be more in keeping with natural evolution for you to wait until your teeth and your genitals grow a little. But there won't be time. I have a better idea. I poured some sweetened condensed milk onto a saucer, drop by drop. Albínka just sniffed it, didn't even take a lick, and walked off, cleaning her mouth and little snout with both paws and fluffing up the fur that had gotten gluey from the sticky sweet stuff. Ruprecht, constantly keeping his eye on his mate, stepped carelessly into the milk and walked off to clean his shoes. Red the Second was the last to walk up to the milk. He took a lick, and kept on licking. We watched in surprise. When he finished the milk I dropped some more on the saucer, and thinned it down with some pure alcohol. Red began to drink some more.

"What are you doing to him now?" said Eva.

"Nothing," I said.

"Don't drink it," Eva shouted at Red, and started to push him away.

But I slapped her hand.

When Red the Second had finished, he skipped away toward Albínka. But Ruprecht bit him in the ear in passing. Red just tossed his head, turned and snapped at Ruprecht, who retreated in surprise. Red started out after Albínka again. He cooed, he wriggled, but she walked away; he followed her but she walked away again; again he followed her; she turned on him angrily, but he cuddled up to her, whereupon she bit him. He didn't mind, it didn't even hurt, and this time he even succeeded in putting his hind legs upon her behind, but she shook him off. When he slid down, he wiped the drop of blood onto her precious side.

That night, long after Vašek and Eva had gone to sleep, I was still working on my computations. What woke me up was my head falling on the table. I wiped the saliva off the state budget

154

and went in to take a look at the guinea pigs, asleep in their residence. Only Pavel's bed was empty. The door to the balcony was shut, and I opened it a little, so the cat could get in. I took my papers in their waterproof wrapping out of the cage and wrote down the events and the thoughts of the day.

Now, having re-read it—and it's almost morning—I observe wanly that the silly banker forgot to write in the third person again. He'll do better tomorrow. I'll see to that.

XVIII

The banker opened his eyes. First thing, he remembered that today he was to do something important; he just couldn't seem to recall what it was supposed to be. He started by going back to yesterday, what he had been doing last thing yesterday. Was it something to do with work, or the children? And then he had it: one of his kids was in the hospital. The third day.

Outside, the sun was shining. Cars were going up and down the streets, lots of high heels were clicking on the cobblestones. What time is it? He stopped short when he saw that his watch had stopped. It said half past six. What business did it have stopping! He shook it and it started ticking again, it still had plenty of power. He got out of bed and opened the door to the neighboring room. In the coolness of the children's room—his oldest son asleep on one bed, the other bed neatly made—a black cat sat in the middle of the floor. It looked at him and cringed. Then it glanced to the balcony door. The wind was billowing the curtain there. The banker quickly backed out of the room and shut the door. "So that's done," he whispered to himself.

He went into his wife's room. She got up in silence and looked

156

at the wall clock. It was half past six. So his watch had only stopped a few seconds earlier, that was apparently what had awakened him.

"Nothing's the matter," said the banker. "Good morning."

"What isn't the matter?" asked Eva, confused.

"Nothing. Except for that cat; it's in there again," he said.

Eva lay down again, exhausted, pale, crumpled. He sat down on the edge of her bed and sat there for a while that way, his hands on his knees. Then he returned to the children's room. The boy was already awake; he was lying on his side with his head on his arm, looking at the cat, which was still sitting there, observing the cage with the skittering guinea pigs. At that point, the guinea pigs began to squeal frantically, because they had heard his footsteps. The banker thought that it was odd that they had been silent the first time he had come into the room. Now they were puling as if their morning hunger were truly painful. But he knew the explanation to this phenomenon: the guinea pigs start to squeal when someone approaches them along Eva's orbit.

"Good morning," said the boy in the bed. "I apparently brought the cat in again."

"That's all right," said the banker. "Take it to bed with you so it doesn't run away."

Vašek dropped his bare feet to the floor and went to get the cat. He picked it up, snuggled it up to his cheek like a pillow. The banker closed the door to the balcony. He poured some seed out for the guinea pigs. The three heads barely fit into the dish. The female with the big tummy was still squealing with hunger as she ground the first seeds of barley between her teeth. She was the hungriest and the prettiest. The large white guinea pig looked like a fat suckling hog, while the little rusty guinea pig resembled nothing so much a bunny rabbit. But she, she was like a graceful young nanny goat or a young girl. All the guinea pigs let themselves be scratched behind the ears as they were eating. In the kitchen, the cat got a saucer of milk.

During breakfast, the conversation got around to being born. Vašek wanted to know how long it took him to be born.

"Nine months," said the banker, intentionally.

"I know that," said the lad, "I mean the really being born part."

"A few hours," said Eva.

"Any ordinary person takes a few hours," the banker said to the lad, "you took two days."

"Is that why you're always so mad at me? I couldn't help it."

"Yes, you could," said the father.

"Could not," said the son.

"Could," repeated the father.

"All right," said the son.

Eva said, "One day we took off for the maternity hospital in a big rush, and it seemed we wouldn't make it in time. Then I just lay around there, one day, two days, and they sent me home. Your dad came and he had to shake me up for half a day in a trolley bus before they would let us back in."

"Oh, so that's the way it was," said Vašek with his mouth full.

"Pavel, he came into the world right away," said Eva. "The doctor went off someplace for a minute, the nurse just turned her head, and I had to catch Pavel so he wouldn't fall. That's how fast he came tumbling out."

"Oh, so that's the way it was," Vašek said again.

"Heaven knows what he's doing now," said Eva.

"Lying there having a fever," said the banker.

"I wonder," said Vašek, "how our little Albínka's going to have her babies."

"Pavel was looking forward to it so much, and now he won't be there," said Eva.

Outside, the sun was shining. It was going to be a lovely day. It was time to go to school and to work. Vašek left at the same time as his mother, although they went to different schools. The banker stayed home, the bank didn't open till nine.

Once he was left alone, he went into the menagerie. First he moved Ruprecht and Albínka from the cage to the maternity ward. He covered them with the drawing board and weighted it down with some books. Then he went back to the kitchen for the cat. As he carried him from the kitchen, he could hear Red the Second crying that he didn't want to be left alone. "You won't be," the banker thought, opened the door a crack and let the tomcat in. "I'd like to see it, but I don't have the time," he said to himself softly.

He went down to the basement and dragged his brand new bicycle, trademarked Favorit, up to the hall. He wondered whether he could manage to lead another bike as he rode the first, and concluded that he couldn't. So he put his own bicycle away again and brought a smaller, three-quarter sized bike, Pavel's, upstairs instead. He raised the seat as high as it would go, locked the basement and rode out into the street.

He had never ridden a bicycle in the city. He wondered whether traffic regulations were the same for him as they were for an automobile or a trolley car. Riding on the bumpy cobblestones was uncomfortable, the cars passing him were frightening, but he probably wasn't allowed to ride on the sidewalks. But it was beautiful out, a pleasant cool wind blew from the park, and on the bridge, the banker hopped off the bike to look down at the sparkling river. He contemplated what he had decided to do, and wondered once again whether it could be done. "Of course, it can," he told himself again. "You can do everything that your mind can happily conjure up in sober theory, and from then on, any objections that crop up in the process, you should suspect of being cowardly ones. Then you should either drop the excellent idea right then and there, or simply not waste your time with any doubts." So he got back onto the bike and proceeded with his plan to save his son, because only he knew how.

The light at the intersection was red. Just to be on the safe side, he stopped. He stared at the ruby light and thought of the creatures hidden under the books. He wondered how far the little black tomcat had come in the process of putting its own determined plan into action. "When I get home," he thought to himself, "Eva's little guinea pig won't be alive any more. He'll be a son of death," he said aloud. "I'd like to see it," he whispered. He's going to the other world, let that gifted little girl play with him there.

He arrived at the hospital, and it was nine o'clock. He surmised that the doctors were just starting their rounds. He rode around the brick walls a couple of times. The bicycle hummed merrily, the spokes rang. He stopped and dropped the seat down low again. He passed under the gateway and leaned the bike against the porter's booth. All he took along was the net shopping bag with the parcel containing the boy's clothes. He headed toward the building. He entered the ground floor along with some attendants who were pushing a cart with cylinders of compressed gas. A nurse emerged from an office; she began a discussion with the men, leading them off someplace to where the gas belongs. The banker glanced into the office through the open door. He removed a white coat from the hanger right by the door, and put it on. As he climbed the stairs, his spine was stiff in the expectation that someone would call him back down. He found a stethoscope in the pocket of the white coat; he hung it around his neck and that calmed him down a little. On the second floor, he walked the entire length of the corridor with a determined stride, examining the room numbers. Some of the doors were open. He heard some crying, some yelling, the consoling voice of a nurse. There were five beds in the corner room, and in the bed right by the door he saw a pale, silent child, lying there, its hands in front of its face, playing with its fingers. At the other end of the corridor, a door opened, some voices emerged into the corridor, followed by a group of people in white, and they entered the next door. He walked into the room and said, "Hi, Pavel. We're going home!"

The boy looked up calmly without saying a word. But he didn't move.

"Well, what is it?" he sat down by him. "You don't want to go home?"

"I do," said the lad. "I'm sick."

"Not any more. Get up and come on."

He took his hand and almost dragged him off the bed. They walked down the corridor together, down the stairs to the ground floor. He took the boy into a waiting room and changed him into the clothes he had brought from home. They left the hospital gown and the doctor's white coat in the waiting room. It was just as simple as the banker had expected. The boy went peacefully, he just straggled behind a little. He squinted and frowned in the sunlight. He said, "I didn't turn in that book, I've got to go back, I didn't give the nurse back her book."

"She'll take it herself."

"But, Dad, I'm sick."

"Maybe, but you'll be well in a couple of hours."

They arrived at the gate. The lad looked at the bike in surprise. He touched it.

"It's nice. But is Albínka going to have her babies, finally?"

"She wanted to have them last night already. But she postponed it so you could be there."

They got home first with the boy pedalling slowly beside his father, and then with the father giving him a lift part of the way. But the banker's state of mind kept falling, the boy seemed not to be himself. And he was almost cold, freezing, and he was perspiring at the forehead. But what could be done, at this point? They stopped off at the school where Eva taught. The boy waited downstairs while the banker went up to leave her a message to come home as soon as she could, because Pavel had come home from the hospital.

Together they put the bike away in the basement. The banker kept waiting for the lad to be amazed at the three other new bikes, but all he did was to say, dryly, "You really pulled one off this time, dad."

It occurred to him that the lad had stopped loving him. Something had happened. Of course, he knew what had happened, for all that, but in addition, something had happened inside the child.

They entered the apartment, and, for the first time, Pavel smiled, a sad and suspicious smile. He was taking off his shoes in the hall, and looking around as if he hadn't been here in ages. The banker thought to himself that he had done it at the very last minute. He was pleased. But what would happen now? Where was the tomcat, and what about the guinea pigs? It was with anxiety that he opened the door to the menagerie. If the

161

rusty guinea pig isn't a son of death, would he have to be the one to do it? He could tell from the doorway that the guinea pig wasn't in its cage.

They never found it. But the black cat was gone too. It never came again.

XIX

Oh, you old warm walls, what will happen when you crumble to rock and brick! Will the crevices in you release what is left of the ideas and the moods of your masons? You, old locomotive wheel, shunted aside onto a rusty track! Cooling and disintegrating, perhaps you too will breathe a sign containing the constructive will of your designer! And, you, dirty timbers of the railyard fence, isn't your mossy surface a protocol of the service of the forest's gamekeeper? And where did the intentions of the passengers roll off to, travellers straining for a change in location, only to—what? And where is it? When decay causes everything to give up its will and wishes like fine wisps of smoke, for whom is the sacrifice being burnt? And what is being asked?

A man strode down the path along the brook, slowly, gazing at everything with the melancholy of someone who is trying to ennoble himself by feeling sorry for everything that is limited by time. "What for? all those papers of mine, and for whom all my nocturnal computations?" he thought sweepingly, when it appeared to him that the day that was ending was beautiful, and that tomorrow there would be a new sun, and tomorrow, and tomorrow . . .

The brilliance of the day was resting slantwise in the valley, one side of the valley was already in the shadow, and people were watering their flower beds. There were names on the gates. Behind the fences daffodils were in blossom, bleeding hearts, pansies and lilacs. The man occasionally turned around, as if he didn't want to relinquish a second glance at what he was passing. He arrived at the viaduct, unreal as it straddled the valley. He stopped and examined it, its stone and its iron. The viaduct framed a view of houses, a picturesque view for the observer. The man stood directly under the viaduct and raised his head. He imagined the collapse of the middle arch of the bridge; he imagined it so vividly that he felt the urge to jump to one side. Dead. Red—he appeared joyful over something, and thought of the way back. Suddenly, his intentions aroused a sensation of distaste. He should turn back. But he didn't turn back, he went on and didn't turn back.

The gate was unlocked, so the man rang the bell. But no one came to open it for him, and so he climbed over the gate, having looked to the left and right. No one saw anyone, and no one was walking down the path to tell him, "oh, no, nobody's home in there! No, the old gentleman went away! Didn't you know? He died! He went to visit his daughter, nobody's home." It was as if it weren't just the city that he had left behind at the viaduct, but everyone else too. Now, if a pillar of fire were to rise above the city, no one would be saved. Nor did anyone welcome him here— there was no one to say hello to, not even the dear weasel.

The door to the cellar was closed with the peg, just like last time. He reached out a hand to take a look, but he changed his mind. "That time you both were here, now I'm alone," he whispered. Rocks.

And Eva! Hey, Eva!

As he unlocked the porch, he thought that is wasn't very pleasant to stand with your back to a cliff with a door in it. One of the keys that he brought with him had to fit. "You're a romantic," he chided himself. "Do what you want to do, just don't keep slipping into emotions." The yard behind him was empty, enclosed. "You say you don't want to be a romantic," he thought with derision, "but you brought your hunting knife, your dagger, like a little boy would." At that point the lock turned and the door opened. He expected an ordinary interior. He saw a wicker armchair with piles and piles of postal receipts.

The next door was also locked. He opened it with the first key that he tried—a lucky coincidence. As he entered, he saw right away the wooden trap door in the floor. He overcame the urge to walk around it and silently walked across it instead. The door to the next room wasn't locked. When he pressed the handle and entered, he found himself in a completely empty room with a deep resonance. There were postal receipts all over the floor. Aside from that, there was nothing else in the room. He went through another room, equally emptied, and found himself in the entrance hall, having made a full circle. There were only two doors left. He assumed that one of them would lead to the kitchen, and the other, he'd know for sure in a moment.

There was nothing left in the kitchen but the cook-stove. The man backed out into the hall. There was only one door left. It was narrower and worse, it didn't have a handle, just a keyhole; he found the key in the bunch he was carrying. As he placed the key in the keyhole, he knew that this was the right door, the one he had come for. He opened it.

All the way back, by the wall, in a dusky corner of the long, narrow cell with its concrete floor, stood a mouldy barrel. It was a mere five steps away. He couldn't take the five steps. He knew what that barrel was for. He didn't need to convince himself. He didn't need to, nor did he want to. He wanted to turn back, quickly and harmlessly, to run out of the house, jump the fence and flee to where there were people, where people were! But the way we doubt a person who is telling us a story that is one hundred per cent true, but too incredible, and the way we reassure ourselves that he is telling the truth by asking him further questions, he knew that if he left here the way his feet would have him do, once he got home, his head wouldn't believe, and it would annoy him: "See, and you didn't convince yourself after all!" And so he took the five steps.

Now he was standing over the barrel, but suddenly he couldn't see it because he was blocking the light. He was just getting ready to reach out and touch the barrel in the dark when he caught its scent, which stopped him. At the same moment, he felt a chill in his loins. My loin! In the narrow door to the concrete room, there must be someone standing there.

He turned and saw him. It was the most dangerous person that he had ever been capable of imagining in all his life, even though he had never met anyone like him. The man smiled with soft fat lips, slid his foot forward so he could reach comfortably into his pocket, and pulled out a pistol. The man did not realize that he was retreating until he felt the calf of his leg touch the rounded and solid wall of the barrel. The pistol was aimed at his belly. "And that's all of it, where I was going," he thought to himself, "with this kind of horror at the end of it? God, the yard would have been better! Here?"

But he knew he deserved it, why, he had out and out asked for it, and he felt himself being executed—though very strictly, certainly not without a just cause or without guilt. The horrible person in the doorway stopped smiling, and his will was visibly concentrating wholly on the pistol that was aimed firmly at the man's gut. "No!" shouted the man inside himself, and he stepped forward.

In order that he might get somewhere, he began to speak, with great effort. He said, "Yes!" and then he continued, in a soft hoarse voice, "Yes, yes sir, please, please! Yes!" He advanced, step by step, and he kept on talking, all the time: "Yes, here, right here! Yes sir!" and he pointed pleadingly at his forehead with his finger and stepped forward, approaching the person whose pistol actually wavered and began to rise. The man noticed it, with delight. "Haaah! Hooo!" he exclaimed suggestively at the marksman, approached the white head and sought for some eyes in the black pits there, eyes that he might grasp with his own eyes, and hang on to. "Hoho!" he said, observing how the skin on that skull was tensing. "Shshshsh!" he hissed with effort at his murderer, who had obediently raised the aim of the pistol all the way to his forehead. Now he could see into the barrel, now he caught a glimpse, in the bottom of the pits, of the cool eyes

166

of his unknown colleague; he grasped them and hung on for a second, and—still pointing to his head with his left hand, shshsh! his right hand rammed the dagger in the person's gut.

The disgusting cool eyes registered surprise, the ugly mouth opened silently to disclose the darkness in the idiot's skull. The pistol fell out of his damned wet hand and struck the concrete. But instead of backing up, the person advanced onto the dagger! And so, out of sheer helplessness, the man sliced open the gut, with a long upward stroke. The heavy body fell forward, insensible, thank God. This is what I've always wished for, ever since I was a boy, thought the man, and he stepped back to let the murderer fall. As he tumbled and fell out of the frame, another, indentical one arose in the doorway. "And that is always the worst of it," the man thought bitterly, and wanted to cry.

At home, the two lads Pavel and Vašek were amusing themselves watching the brand new guinea pigs. They had been born at noon and no one had been watching. Pavel had been reading and didn't realize that the mother-to-be was squeaking restlessly. When he looked at her, three little young ones were running around Albínka, sticking their tiny heads into her tummy, looking to get their beestings. One of the guinea pigs was white with a black head, the second was rusty with white cheeks, and the third, grey like a hare. None of them was all white like its daddy, at least, if not like its mommy.

The guinea pigs knew how to run around, even at the age of less than six hours; they knew how to scratch behind their ears, wash their mouths and squeak quite passably.

Children dear! "And Pavel," said Eva, "are you sure nothing hurts you?"

"Sure," he replied.

"But where could he be so long?" Eva wondered.

"He'll come," said Vašek.

"Won't he be surprised that not a single one is white?" said Pavel.

"But why doesn't he come?" repeated Eva.

"He'll come," repeated Vašek.

But he never came and they never heard of him again.

167